A DISTANT HEART

ALSO BY HEATHER BLANTON

Grace Be a Lady

Hell-Bent on Blessings

A Scout for Skylar

Locket Full of Love

Carolina Homecoming

A Good Man Comes Around

Romance in the Rockies Series

A Lady in Defiance

Hearts In Defiance

A Promise In Defiance

Daughter of Defiance

A Destiny in Defiance

Hope in Defiance

A Reckoning in Defiance

In Time For Christmas: A Novella

A DISTANT HEART

A SWEET WESTERN CHRISTIAN ROMANCE

BURNING DRESS RANCH
BOOK ONE

HEATHER BLANTON

A Distant Heart
Paperback Edition

CKN Christian Publishing
An Imprint of Wolfpack Publishing
1707 E. Diana Street
Tampa, FL 33610

www.cknchristianpublishing.com

First edition published in 2020.

Paperback ISBN 979-8-89567-840-4 Ebook ISBN 979-8-89567-839-8

AUTHOR'S NOTE

Are you dumb? Are you worthless? Why can't you ever do anything right? I don't know why I bother with you...

Too, too many of you have shared with me the incredible, hurtful things your husbands—and now mostly EX-husbands—have said to you. Amazing, isn't it, the wounds mere words can inflict? I know a little something about this as well. So, I wanted to write a story that gave a voice to our pain and, I pray, helps us get our eyes on things above. Remember: You are fearfully and wonderfully made. The God of the universe sings over you with joy! He loves you, He fights for you—you are precious to Him. Precious. Never forget that! I hope *A Distant Heart* points you back to these FACTS.

On a lighter note, my daddy used to tell me that I could do anything I put my mind to. He instilled a lot of confidence in me—truly made me believe in myself. That is probably why it was so jarring the first few times I collided with men who thought I was incapable of something simply because of my gender.

Don't get me wrong. I'm no feminist. God made us the weaker vessel, but sometimes we are stronger than the men around us. Sometimes, on the other hand, the men around us respect the differences between male and female and let us soar because of those differences—not in spite of them.

Burning Dress Ranch was inspired by two very odd and different things, the first being Fantasy Island. Yes, the old TV show captained by the mysterious Mr. Roarke, played to perfection by the exquisitely handsome Ricardo Montalbán. There was a story behind his character that was never spelled out, but it seemed he had a special connection with the heavenly realm. Or so I thought. I often wondered what wonderful stories could have been written if, instead of an island, he'd run a cattle ranch—because I think that about every TV show, character, and actor.

Second, the idea for the ranch itself came from the inimitable and famous Buckley sisters.

Eastern Montana is, in my opinion, one of the most beautiful and lonely places in the US. It is not an area for the faint of heart. The weather, the wide-open spaces, the solitude...it's the kind of place that makes you or breaks you.

This is why the story of May, Myrtle, and Mabel Buckley is all the more remarkable.

When Franklin and Susannah Buckley started having children, surely they had hoped for boys. After all, farming in the Dakotas and ranching in Montana was man's work. But the Buckley daughters were born for this land. Franklin was smart enough to know it…or perhaps his precocious, fearless, ambitious daughters gave him no choice. They bloomed on those prairies like wildflowers after a snowy winter. They took to the saddle as if they'd been born to it. Their father's ranch hands taught the girls to ride, rope, shoot, brand, round up, even break broncs, and called them, with affection, the Red Yearlings.

Confident in his daughters' abilities, Franklin turned his 160-acre ranch in Terry, Montana, over to the girls. This freed him up to manage the farm in North Dakota, other business ventures, and serve as a state representative. Papa was also confident that men would be men, especially where his three pretty daughters were concerned. Hence, he did not leave them unattended. The girls' mother stayed close, keeping a watchful eye on her lovely Red Yearlings.

In 1914, neighbor and friend Evelyn Cameron photographed the girls working and playing on the ranch. Cameron wrote an article about Montana cowgirls and featured the feisty ranching sisters doing what they did best. While this article spread their fame to Europe, the girls had already been fielding invitations from Wild West shows and even President Roosevelt. Turned 'em all down flat. May, Myrtle, and Mabel were ranchers. The profession was no game to them. The most play-acting they did was posing for the now-famous and very collectible Cameron photos.

I'd like to point out, they did all this in skirts. Oh,

there was a brief scandal whereby the girls tried wearing *split* skirts. Apparently, Montana was not ready for culottes. The lady photographer was even threatened once with arrest over in Miles City for wearing the things. So, the girls went back to skirts, wearing said culottes when nobody was looking.

May, the oldest of the sisters, never married. The more reserved of the three, she nursed her mother for years after a stroke, then died at only fifty years of age.

Myrtle, the middle sister, was a handful. One could guess she occasionally had bouts of the *Marsha, Marsha, Marsha* syndrome. She eloped with a ranch hand and had two children with him. The marriage failed, and Myrtle later married rancher and neighbor George Straugh. That one stuck.

Mabel married Milton Gile and lived to a ripe old age.

I'm telling you about the Buckley sisters because they did, in fact, run successful ranching operations that were the envy of the male-dominated industry.

If you believe, you can achieve. Because with God, all things are possible.

A DISTANT HEART

PROLOGUE

"Oh, Father, not him. Please give him a second chance. He just fell in with the wrong crowd. If he'd had time to think, he never would have even been there. I believe in him. I love him. Please give him a second chance. He'll change, I'm sure of it."

What if he doesn't, my child?

"He will, I know he will. He's good at his core. I know it."

He deserves judgment. Like the others.

"But would you show him mercy simply because your daughter asks it?"

CHAPTER ONE

"YOU WAITIN' ON ANOTHER *PETTICOAT*?"

The mocking, gravelly voice interrupted Jax Taylor's survey of the empty train tracks. He held his face still and slid his gaze over to Bob Woodward. "Yep," he answered flatly, shifting on the wagon seat and ignoring the insult.

The foreman at the Bar T, Woodward, was a lean, pockmarked mongrel from somewhere down in Florida. Always looking for trouble, too, it seemed. He wore a bullwhip at his side and was rumored to be downright deadly with it, though Jax had yet to see the man use it. Grinning now like his wit was as fast as the whip, Woodward leaned back on the train station's wall and began unraveling the lash.

Buddy Haekstrom stepped out of the depot office and nodded at Jax. "So, you know anything about this one?" A spry man for his seventy years, he was as nosy as Woodward, but not as annoying. In fact, Jax enjoyed his chats with the old man as they waited on the new hands for the Burning Dress. By now, though, the clerk knew better than to ask questions.

"Nope," Jax said flatly. "And you know I ain't at liberty to discuss it."

The old man scratched his chin and exchanged a disappointed glance with Woodward. Jax could guess at the stories and theories percolating in the old man's brain. His pale green eyes glimmered with foolish notions.

Woodward drew a bead on something Jax couldn't see and popped the whip. A beetle shot up into the air, cut cleanly in half.

Buddy shoved his hands into his pockets and rocked on his heels. "That's pretty good, Woodward."

"It's a hobby."

He coiled the whip back to a circle, and Buddy returned his attention to Jax. "You know, funny how they get off the train, or step down from the stage, and just look like life has beat the hound out of 'em. They're all bent over, quiet, don't meet your gaze. And then…" He trailed off, staring down the track. The train whistle drifted softly to them.

"And then?" Jax asked, curious himself what the old man was thinking.

"They leave. But they ain't the same. Their chins are up, their backs are straight, they even speak to me. Never tell me where they're going or what happened out there at Burning Dress…but—"

"But they're different, that's for sure," Woodward said, replacing the whip on his belt. "I've heard about strange goings-on out there, Jax." Woodward's brow ticked up, suggesting dark and inappropriate ideas. "What are you doing to those gals?"

Jax removed his hat and raked his fingers through black, sweaty curls, all while eyeing Woodward with weary annoyance. The man never let up, never just let things pass. He was intent on making his mark on both the Bar T and Jax. "Woodward, you ain't the one filling the town with crazy stories, are you?" He dropped his hat back in place. "Doc actually asked me if the girls are dancing around the fire at night naked." And that was just one of the cock-and-bull stories Jax had heard. "You know, if I thought you were the one spreading that manure"—he dropped his voice—"I'd have to quit being polite to you."

The old man's eyes just about bugged out of his skull. Woodward's eyes narrowed. "No, I ain't never said nothing like that." He folded his arms across his chest. "Any truth to it?" He wiggled his eyebrows.

Jax wanted to spit. He shot the foreman a hard, warning glare. One day, he was going to have to straighten Woodward out on a few things. "I'll tell you what the truth is. Miss Sally is a good, God-fearing woman. What she does out there is help. She —" He clamped his jaw down. He was sorely tempted to give Woodward an earful, but bit it all back. Miss Sally had given him and the other boys clear instructions to say as little as possible about her ranch. People had been dismissed for saying too much. And the last thing Jax wanted was to go back to the Bar T with his tail between his legs. "You don't have enough to keep you busy at the Bar T? Gotta worry about a bunch of women showing you how to ranch?"

Woodward came off the wall. Jax held the man's challenging stare. If there had to be a fight, he was ready, but he preferred not to tangle with this particular skunk today. The train whistled again, much louder this time, and Jax took it as an excuse to turn away from the man. "Stick to your own, Woodward."

The locomotive glided into the station in a mass of steam and screaming brakes. In a few minutes, Buddy had the step in place and passengers began spilling forth. Woodward greeted a man in a suit and the two ambled back toward town together. Jax tapped his fingers on his thigh, wondering why his charges always disembarked last. He knew exactly what he was looking for, just not the exact woman.

He found it interesting that Buddy had been smart enough to peg Miss Sally's new ranch hands. Even more so, their transformation. The old man was pretty eagle-eyed.

And when Cecelia Huggins stepped down from the train, Jax again agreed Buddy's observation had been on the money. Miss Huggins—or was it Mrs.?—lit on the platform with the fluid grace of a wary cougar. Clutching a scarred leather suitcase at her side, she scanned the platform with a suspicious gaze and defiant lift to her head. Wearing a green dress that matched her eyes, he couldn't help noticing she was a pretty thing, light and petite but curvy. Wavy auburn hair pulled back from her face revealed high cheekbones, dark, thick lashes outlining those striking green eyes, and the tiniest scar above her otherwise flawless, pink lips.

But he'd come to the hard-won conclusion that the prettier they were, the more hell they wreaked on a man, which was why he was such a good fit for the Burning Dress.

He locked the brake, jumped to the platform, and slowly approached her. When these gals first got here, they tended to be jumpy as rabbits and suspicious as whipped dogs. "Miss Huggins?"

She turned. Wisps of fine, russet hair loosened from her ribbon drifted across her lips. Her mouth opened in what he thought at first was fear, but the slightest curl to her lip pointed him more toward disdain. A little bewildered by her reaction, Jax quickly lifted his hand. "I'm Jax Taylor. I'm here to take you out to Burning Dress."

THE DRIVE WASN'T ALL that long out to the ranch, but too often it was awkward. These girls never had much to say, especially about themselves. It was always obvious they were recovering from some soul-scarring event. Sometimes the scars were visible. Occasionally, they would try to ask questions about Burning Dress. Why had they been invited here? Was it really a ranch? Who was this mysterious Miss Sally?

Jax gave them all the same speech, as he did now to Miss Huggins. "I'm Miss Sally's foreman. I run the ranch. We have four thousand head. You'll know the boss by her long, silver braid." Every now and then, depending on how the young lady struck him, he might add, *"You don't need to be afraid. It's a safe place."* Today, he did not say that to the woman beside him, clutching her valise in front of her so tightly her fingers were white.

Cecelia Huggins was a little afraid, he thought, but mostly she seemed determined. Determined to do what, he wasn't sure. Tiny, angry lines etched themselves into the corners of her eyes as she stared out at the distant Wind River range. He didn't think she saw the craggy mountains at all. The tension in her brow, the tight, thin line of her lips betrayed bitter ruminations. That's why he wasn't surprised when she asked, "I understand the ranch, or whatever it is, is mostly run by women. Is that true?"

"Yes, ma'am. Just a handful of us men there."

She took her gaze back to the mountains. "Good."

CECELIA'S PETITE, black boots clicked too loudly on the stone floor and she softened her steps. The main hall in the ranch house was wide and framed with shimmering log walls hung with wrought iron sconces. A mammoth log staircase with open treads led up to the second floor. She stepped to her left and peered into a parlor adorned with leather furniture, a giant stone fireplace, and animal trophies on the walls. No humans occupied the room, however. Sweaty fingers clutching her satchel, she stepped gingerly to the other side of the hall. A dark, paneled door was slightly ajar. She moved closer and peeked in.

A woman with long, silver hair plaited down her shoulder was studiously writing in a ledger. The cowboy who had picked her up in town—Jax, was it? —had said she would know Miss Sally by the braid, if nothing else. He'd been kind enough to keep conversation to a minimum, explaining she should hold her questions for the boss.

Cecilia moistened her lips and rapped lightly on the door.

"Come."

She took a deep breath and entered the high-ceilinged library. An instant later, she met the stunning, piercing violet eyes of the *boss*. Dressed like a man in pants and a vest, the woman rose, laying down her pencil as she did, and openly surveyed Cecelia. Her stoic expression, however, gave way quickly to a warm smile. "Cecelia Huggins, I presume?"

"Yes, ma'am." How did she know? "I'm sorry, I'm a few days earlier than—"

"I'm Miss Sally. And not to worry, your accommodations are ready. Please, have a seat." With a graceful sweep of her hand, she motioned to the chairs facing her desk.

"Thank you." Cecelia settled into a large wingback leather chair, dropping her dusty suitcase on the oriental rug. Miss Sally was a conundrum. Dressed like a man, yet the woman moved with the lithe, polished elegance of a duchess.

"Reverend Springer shared very little of your story with me," she began, "other than you are a good fit for Burning Dress Ranch. Can you tell me why he thought that?"

Cecelia shook her head, uncomfortable with how little she knew of this place or this woman. "Essentially, that's what he told me. I could think here, make some future plans." Reverend Springer had merely told her Burning Dress was the place for her to think, plan...heal.

Miss Sally picked up the pencil again and tapped it on the ledger as she seemed to ponder Cecelia, who pondered her right back. Miss Sally was a slender, beautiful woman, perhaps in her early fifties. Confidence and strength emanated from her like a fragrance, and Cecelia found her anxiety fading and her willingness to explain things growing. "My husband has divorced me. We discovered I cannot have children because of a deformity to my uterus."

"And he ended the marriage to you over the issue?" The woman sounded neither startled nor angry.

"Yes. He said I lied to him about my suitability and capabilities as a wife."

"Did you lie?"

"No, I had no idea."

"And he turned you out?"

"He threw a handful of garments into this case, including my wedding gown, tossed it out on the sidewalk in front of our home in Atlanta, and then pushed me out the door right behind it." Unexpectedly, Cecelia's throat tightened, and she clamped her teeth together. A wife discarded like a worn rug. The memory was painful, to be sure, especially the way William had punctuated it with a slamming door. What had hurt nearly as badly were the blinds and shutters closing in rapid succession on the nearby homes. So they wouldn't see. Friends and neighbors who had turned their backs on her. As if she had a scarlet letter branded on her forehead. "I stayed at the church. In the wing with unwed mothers, ironically."

Miss Sally smirked but wiped it away almost instantly. "How long were you married?"

"Four years."

"Do you have any special skills, talents, gifts of any kind?"

The change in subject left Cecelia sputtering for a moment. "Um…" She decided she wanted some answers and leaned forward. "Can you tell me why I'm here?"

"That's what I'm trying to find out. I can't help every woman who shows up on my doorstep."

"I'm sorry, I don't understand. I thought this was a ranch. Is it some sort of hospital or sanitarium?"

Miss Sally cut loose with a rich, musical laugh. "Oh, Lord, Burning Dress Ranch is a lot of things, but sanitarium isn't one of them." She leaned back in her chair and laced long, elegant fingers over her stomach. "You've come here to polish a trade or skill. If you don't have one, you'll learn one. Then, at some time in the future, you'll decide whether you're staying on or going back into the world to make your way."

Right now, the last thing Cecelia wanted to see was the world. "I sew."

"You any good?"

"Very good. And I keep house well."

Miss Sally shrugged. "Got housekeeping staff. Good seamstresses keeping our people clothed."

"I was a teacher for a spell. I'm fluent in French and German."

Miss Sally scratched her chin. "Not much call for a translator right now. Anything else?"

"I also enjoy gardening, and I'm good with animals."

"Animals. Can you ride horses?"

"Well, I'm probably a touch rusty, but I did grow up on a farm in Virginia."

"Rusty?" A glint came into the woman's eyes, as if she were glad to hear of a weakness in Cecelia's resumé. "We can always use another hand with the cattle. Always. It's hard work, though."

Cecelia pondered the unexpected and outlandish idea. Good, satisfying, hard work, outdoors, mercifully brief interactions with other humans, but it was man's work—

"You'll learn to ride, rope, and brand, and manage the stock. When you leave, you can work at any ranch in the country, if you're of a mind to."

"But I'm a woman!" Cecelia was incredulous.

Miss Sally's mouth ticked up in the corner, expressing a little annoyance. "I gathered as much. Miss Huggins—Cecelia—my *graduates* are highly sought after. You might not be the strongest cowboy physically, but when you leave Burning Dress, you will be among the best." Her tone brooked no argument.

"Graduates? So, this is a type of school?"

"You can say that." She rose and seemed to almost glide around to Cecelia. "You see, one of my goals is to make sure every woman here leaves with a skillset she can use to take care of herself. So she's never at the mercy of a man again." An elegant hand floated up and she motioned toward the door. "Let me show you around."

Miss Sally led Cecelia to the second floor and stopped at the top of the stairs. A long hallway stretched out before them, two doors on each side. She went to the first door on the left and opened it. "These are your accommodations."

Cecelia peeked in. It was a large, open room with two support pillars in the center and two rows of four bunk beds. The stone fireplace continued up here, housing another fireplace that probably warmed the area well. Miss Sally ushered her in and they strolled down the center. All the beds were covered in quilts and fluffy pillows. Beside them, a nightstand reflected something unique about the residents, from family photos to books, Bibles, and cards. Trunks of various sizes and descriptions occupied the space at the foot of the bed—from simple foot lockers to large, ornate steamer trunks.

"All of the residents have a job to do," Miss Sally continued. "Some, like you, are learning a skill. Some teach."

"So, Burning Dress *is* a sort of…healing place?" She purposely avoided using the word sanitarium. "You want to teach us to rely on ourselves, stand on our own two feet." The blessed idea of independence…solitude…never bothering with love or friendship again. Life from a distance. Right now, it sounded like heaven.

"This will be yours." They stopped at the last bunk on the right, closest to the fireplace, and Miss Sally pointed to the lower bed. "And, no, learning to *rely* on yourself isn't exactly the goal. I pray your time at Burning Dress will give you two things. First, the ability to support yourself financially. When a woman has that fear removed from her view, she tends to see things more clearly, make better choices. Second, the willingness to forgive those who have wronged you, given you a reason to be here. Bitterness and unforgiveness are heavy chains."

Cecelia grimaced, immediately worried the ranch was some sort of strict religious organization. She was not bitter and, though she didn't ever want to see William again, she didn't hate him. In fact, she was sure in time, something *like* forgiveness would surface. For now, she simply…what? She stumbled over the answer. Had forced the pain he'd caused her into a dark closet? That would do.

Miss Sally inclined her head at Cecelia. An odd, almost *knowing* expression on her face. "There's time for that. Right now, I'd like you to go to that wardrobe." She pointed behind Cecelia at a large oak closet in the corner. "Find a pair of dungarees and a shirt that fits and come back to my office when you're dressed. I think we can squeeze in a quick tour before supper."

SALLY PULLED the door shut behind her, then rested her hand on the knob and shook her head. *Oh, Lord, all these women break my heart, but Cecelia...she's buried her bitterness so deep, even she can't find it now. Those bones, though, always poke through the soil eventually.*

With that determined streak of hers, she's liable to go through a lot of needless hurt before she figures it out...if she figures it out—

But that sounded like doubt, and she repented instantly.

I'm sorry, Lord. With You, all things are possible. You'd think I'd know that by now. Just help me, Holy Spirit, to be especially sensitive to her needs.

I mess this up, the dirt on her heart will turn to cement. I've got to hear Your voice, Father. Every syllable, every instruction is going to matter with this girl.

The still, small voice reminded her gently, *After all this time, my daughter, you know my voice when you hear it. Don't be anxious about anything.*

Peace entered Sally's soul, and she laughed. "Yes, I suppose I *was* fretting. Forgive my foolishness, Father, please." She patted the doorknob lightly and walked away. "It will be all right. It always is."

When the door shut and Cecelia was alone, she heaved a huge sigh and tossed her bag onto the bed. She had no idea what she'd gotten into, but Reverend Springer had seemed adamant that Burning Dress was the place for a divorced and homeless woman. After all, she couldn't continue living at the church. And she had to have some plan for going forward.

To his credit, the reverend had attempted to counsel her husband, but William had passionately refused to let Cecelia return home. He was done with her, divorce being his singular goal. He made no secret he wanted to remarry while he was still young and could father children.

With the covenant broken by hardness of heart, Reverend Springer had thrown up his hands. Burning Dress Ranch, he had said, would be a fine place for Cecelia to heal from her husband's rejection. Perhaps she would also find the love of One who would never leave her or forsake her.

Cecelia struggled with that. Her husband had thrown her out in the blink of an eye. In the next blink, her friends had turned away from her. She suspected the reverend had sent her here simply to get her out of the church's basement. She had no reason to believe Jesus was any more concerned with her than all those other fine citizens.

Love, divine or otherwise, was only a weak, fraying thread spun about people for convenience. Broken and tossed aside when it became inconvenient. She'd vowed to avoid it altogether.

She did, however, like this idea of ranch work.

That was rather exciting. She had initially believed her only options to be either menial housework or teaching again. Cecilia had never really enjoyed the profession, had merely gone into it because her mother had been a teacher.

She missed her mother. She had warned Cecelia about William just before her stroke. She'd said he had a hard, unyielding heart. Oh, how right she had been...

Angrily shaking off the melancholy that threatened to burst through her mental dam, Cecelia strode to the wardrobe and flung open its doors. To her amazement, the shelves were stacked high with dungarees and flannel shirts. She ran her fingers over the tough denim.

Miss Sally had truly meant for Cecelia to put these on? The idea was scandalous—

The thought brought her chin up, prodded at the rebel in her fighting for freedom. Yes, wouldn't this just scandalize William if he ever found out? His worthless, discarded wife bandying about in men's trousers? She snatched a pair off the shelf.

Three attempts later, Cecelia was wearing dungarees that weren't too big in the waist, only a little long in the leg. She cuffed them and stood up. Intrigued by the odd feeling of pants, she bent over, squatted down, twisted, raised her knees high. Her movements were so unhindered. No wonder men wore pants.

And what a sorry commentary on women's lives, that they were forbidden something as useful as trousers, and were instead relegated to hideous, ugly bloomers.

The bottom shelf of the wardrobe contained half a dozen pairs of boots. She picked one up and assessed its condition. Used, but cleaned and oiled. The heels looked to be new, though, and untried, as of yet. Cecelia tried on all six. The last pair fit perfectly.

"Well..." She spun, surveying the dormitory for a mirror. One had been hung on the back of the door. A little hesitantly, she walked the thirty or so feet toward it, watching her image grow. She turned side to side, pivoted away from the glass and looked over her shoulder at her backside. She had a waist, hips, and curves. She still had her hair pulled back and would leave it. Perhaps later she would adopt the braid.

She raised her arms, kicked her legs, and laughed. All this freedom to move. No skirts tangling around her legs. No corset constricting her breathing. Yes, Burning Dress might do after all.

Whatever that meant.

"HOW DO THEY FEEL?"

Cecelia tugged at her waist, slapped her thighs as she approached Miss Sally's desk. "Thus far, quite comfortable."

"Good."

"Though I will admit, for a moment there, as I was coming down the steps, I was afraid this was a prank."

"No prank. If you're going to work outdoors doing a man's job, you'll have the freedom to dress like a man. This Victorian prudishness about women in trousers is absurd. And I'm thoroughly convinced bloomers were designed by Satan himself."

Cecelia laughed and enjoyed the sound of it. "I was thinking almost that exactly."

"You can wear a dress anytime. For working, however, I suggest you stick with the pants. Or bombachas, if you like."

"Bombachas?"

"The gauchos wear them. Pleated, loose-fitting trousers. A touch more feminine." Miss Sally rose. "Now, let's show you Burning Dress. We'll start with the kitchen."

THE ROOM WAS a beehive of activity. Six women—five younger, and one older, portly matron with gray hair—bustled about like ants. They were busy removing biscuits from the oven, shoving in a loaf of dough, slicing vegetables, peeling potatoes, stirring something steaming and savory at the stove, and frying chicken. Everyone was engaged and focused on her particular task. The wonderful odors of herbs, bread, and meat made Cecilia's stomach grumble.

"Maude," Miss Sally said softly, and the activity came to a halt. Half a dozen pairs of eyes landed on Cecelia.

The older woman wiped her hands on a towel and came over to greet them. "Afternoon, Miss Sally."

"Maude, this is our newest hand, Cecelia Huggins. Cecelia, Maude is our head cook."

Loose gray hairs poked every which way from the woman's French twist, and her cheeks were flushed from the kitchen's heat, but she smiled warmly at the guests and their intrusion. "Cecelia."

Cecelia nodded and smiled back. "Maude, it's nice to meet you."

"You cook?"

"I'm assigning her to ranch hand," Miss Sally interjected.

"Oh, well." Maude's head bobbed in approval. "Women who can sit the saddle. Not enough of them. Jax'll be glad to have ya."

Miss Sally then quickly introduced the other girls, but none of their names stuck in Cecelia's head. They were in their mid-twenties, early thirties, ran the gamut from fair-skinned European to Negro to Hispanic. A few smiled with sincere welcome in their expressions. A few seemed only to be politely bored by her.

Just outside the kitchen, another two young ladies were digging up carrots from the small garden, protected from the summer's late afternoon heat by the main house's long shadow. Miss Sally introduced them all, explaining to Cecelia, "This is just a small kitchen garden. We have several acres down by the river planted in corn, wheat, beets, squash, potatoes, and green beans. When it comes to food, Burning Dress is entirely self-reliant."

They rounded the corner, and Cecelia found herself in the midst of a real working ranch. Two cowboys and two female ranch hands astride horses trotted by, a string of Morgans in tow, a dust cloud following. From out on the hills, the definite, but faint cries of cattle mixed with the sounds of whooping cowboys and cracking whips. Hammers, humming saws, and the thud of dropped lumber came from somewhere, perhaps behind the barn.

As Miss Sally strode on, chickens skittered out of her way, and a bleating goat jogged past them. Cecelia lengthened her step to keep up with the tall woman. They seemed to be heading toward the mammoth barn. "It's lively," Cecelia observed. "Tell me, why is it called Burning Dress Ranch?"

Miss Sally slowed her step but didn't stop. "You'll get some answers tonight at supper. We have something special planned."

They veered away from the barn, cutting to the left, toward a small building that looked like a house, though it was so small it could only be one room. Clapboard siding, it had two large windows across the front, a black pipe jutting from the roof, and an open porch. The door was ajar, letting in the fading sun. Cecelia caught sight of a feminine figure passing in front of the opening. At least, she thought she'd noticed long hair and curves, but the person was in pants, too.

"Virginia," Miss Sally called, climbing the front steps. "I've brought our newest guest."

A woman with wide, curious dark eyes and two long black braids met them at the door. She was holding a stout sewing needle threaded with catgut, and like Cecelia and Miss Sally, was also wearing rugged men's attire. "Howdy, Miss Sally."

Cecelia thought immediately she wouldn't call the girl pretty so much as unusual-looking. She had rather long features, full lips, thick lashes, and her expression with those round eyes seemed to be one of near astonishment. She flashed a huge grin at Cecelia and grabbed her hand for a vigorous shake. "I'm Virginia. I do some tack and gear repair. I'm learnin' to make saddles."

Noting Virginia's heavy Southern accent, Cecelia pulled out of the handshake, flexing crushed fingers. "I'm sure you'll be very good at it." *With a grip like that, sewing leather shouldn't be any problem.*

"Like you, Virginia sews, but when Millicent, our saddle maker, decided to leave, she took on training Virginia. Besides sewing, Virginia, Cecelia also rides a little. I decided to put her with Jax's crew."

"Oh, say, that's swell," Virginia agreed with a bobbing head. "Jax is always short-handed. Where you from, 'Celia?"

No one had ever called her by the moniker before, and, for a moment, Cecelia didn't know how to receive it. Virginia, however, beamed at her rather like a happy dog expecting a pat on the head. Cecelia had no intention of making friends with this girl, but she did find the nickname almost endearing. William had never once called her anything but her given name. Until the end. When he'd become fond of calling her *worthless* and *a failure of womanhood*.

"I am lately from Atlanta, but I grew up near Richmond."

"Aw, yeah, thought I heard a dusting of moonlight and magnolia in your accent. I'm from Tennessee." She pointed at herself with evident pride. "Near Dinwiddie, up in the mountains."

For some reason, none of this information surprised Cecelia. "It's lovely to meet you."

As they walked away, Miss Sally chuckled. "Virginia is an infinite bubbling stream of cheerfulness. But she's also what I would call *intuitive* about her personality. She seems to know who can tolerate her and who quickly gets chafed by her."

"That's a priceless gift," Cecelia half-mumbled, half-grumbled.

Miss Sally cut her eyes at Cecelia. "I wonder which you will be? Tolerant or chafed?"

Cecelia thought it was rather obvious, but refrained from saying so.

"All right, one last stop before we go in for supper."

They headed out behind the barn. Off about a hundred yards, a crew of three women were working on what looked like a chicken coop. Rolls of chicken wire lay off to the side. While two of the women were on ladders hammering shingles, the third woman, a tall, muscular black woman, was sawing lumber at the sawhorses. As Miss Sally and Cecelia approached, she ceased her work and straightened up, wiping a hand across her sweaty brow. The edge of the bandana encasing her hair was stained with moisture as well. Though laboring hard, a broad smile expressed a fine mood.

"Miss Sally, how you doin' today?"

"I am blessed and highly favored. And you?"

The woman laughed with joy. "Oh, amen. Me, too, me too."

"Tallulah, I'm taking our newest hand around. This is Cecelia Huggins."

Cecelia offered her hand. "How do you do?"

Tallulah had to switch the saw to the other hand to accept the handshake. "I do all right," she said with conviction. "It's nice to meet you."

"Likewise." Cecelia flexed her fingers, amazed at yet another stout grip.

"Everything is set for tonight, Tallulah." Miss Sally tilted her head and touched the woman's shoulder gently. "You're still ready?"

"Oh, yes, ma'am." The woman seemed to nearly quiver with joy or excitement. "Just sorry I waited this long to come home."

"So long as you did."

The two women hugged, and then Miss Sally began walking away. Cecelia nodded at Tallulah and followed her *boss*.

"Well, that's everything," Miss Sally said, "except for the barn and the livestock. I'll leave all that to Jax to get you settled in. Wander around if you like and then join us in the dining room at seven sharp." She turned to go, but stopped and pivoted back to Cecelia. "If you see Jax, go ahead and give him a heads up, you're signing on to be one of his hands."

Cecelia bit her bottom lip. She'd barely looked at the man, she'd been so preoccupied by the mystery of Burning Dress and what to expect. "He's tall… slender…?"

Miss Sally's brow knit together. "You don't remember what Jax looks like? Lord, you're the first. For most of the girls, he's the *only* thing they remember on their way out here." She shrugged a shoulder. "Anyway, yes, he's tall, slender—but it's lean muscle—he's got blue eyes that can melt a rattlesnake —so I'm told"—she winked—"and a nice, thick head of black hair." She snapped her fingers. "And if you're still not sure, he wears his daddy's Seventh Cavalry pin on his hat."

IN THE LONG, low light of the afternoon sun, Cecelia gravitated away from the busier part of the ranch and found herself standing at a small corral. Inside it, a lone cowboy was brushing a horse down with a looped rope. Dressed in a black shirt and black dungarees, he wore his hat pulled low to block the setting sun and worked with his back to Cecelia. Broad, strong shoulders rippled beneath the cotton work shirt.

He carried on an easy conversation with the mare, using pleasant, calming tones as he dragged the coiled rope up and down her, brushed it over her legs, rubbed her face with it. After several minutes, he slowly unraveled it, made a larger loop, and pulled it over her neck. When she didn't fight this, he slipped it off and then dragged it across her hind quarters.

The horse tolerated these motions with bored switches of her tail. Coiling the rope, the cowboy patted the horse on the neck and praised her. "That's a good girl, Bella. Good girl." He slipped the rope up his arm and hung it on his shoulder. "You're coming along just fine." He took hold of her halter. "And that's enough for today." He started walking her toward the gate when he paused. Most of his face still hidden by the hat, he turned toward Cecelia. "Miss Huggins, isn't it?"

"Yes." The pin on his hat glinted in the sunlight.

He walked over to her, leading Bella. When he reached the fence, he raised his head a touch more, and a stunning pair of azure eyes hit Cecelia full force. They were, indeed, breathtaking, and she wondered how she'd managed to miss them only a few hours before.

"I'm Jax—"

"Yes, I remember. Miss Sally told me to tell you I'll be joining your crew."

Surprise lifted his brow. "You ride?"

"I haven't in a while, but I grew up on a horse." She ducked her chin. "And a farm."

"So, you've been around cattle, too?"

"Dairy cows."

He smiled, revealing gleaming teeth. *Oh, yes,* she thought, *no wonder ladies noticed him.*

"I tell you," he said, "I'll be awfully grateful if you can ride and herd. Can you rope?"

"No. Not with any real skill anyway."

"Sounds like there might be a little experience there. And I can work with that. I'm training Bella here." He scratched the mare's nose. "Gettin' her used to the rope. She made a lot of progress today."

"It looked like it."

A sudden, high-pitched clanging reverberated around the ranch and Cecelia looked toward the main house, the source of the noise. Jax backed the horse away from the fence. "The warning bell. Supper in fifteen. I'll see you here in the morning, Miss Huggins," he said, touching his hat.

She pushed off the fence and nodded her own goodbye, eager to finally find out something of Burning Dress Ranch's mysteries.

CHAPTER TWO

Cecelia assumed the dining room was near the kitchen. To find it, she cut through, returning a nod from a harried Maude, and followed a girl carrying a tray stacked high with fried chicken. They stepped into a space larger than most dining rooms, but perhaps not quite large enough to be called a dining hall. Three rows of three long tables, set for service, ran the length of the room. No one seat looked more important than another, so Cecelia sat at the end of the first table she came to.

The girl set the chicken down in front of her, and Cecelia suddenly wondered if she was being rude. "Can I help with anything?"

"Oh, no, just make yourself comfortable."

Fidgeting, Cecelia picked up a butter knife, breathed on it, and wiped it on her sleeve.

"What's the matter, you don't think they wash the dishes?" Virginia plopped down beside her, the grin and surprised look present.

"N-no," Cecelia stuttered. "Just bored."

Although as she said this, she became aware of women filtering in, their chattering filling the room and rising in volume as they took their seats. Virginia looked up and waved at someone. "Wilhelma, come here. Want ya to meet somebody new."

A big, strapping blonde girl, about twenty or so, waved back and headed toward them. Cecelia thought she recalled her being one of the crew putting shingles on the chicken coop's roof. The girl dropped down opposite them, but Cecelia noted she left the last seat on that side of the table open.

"Cecelia, this here is Wilhelma. She's on the carpentry crew. Wilhelma, meet Cecelia."

The girl jutted out a hand the size of a bear paw. "Yah, it is good to meet you, Cecelia."

Cecelia caught the heavy, German intonations in the girl's accent. "*Guten Abend.*"

Wilhelma gasped. "*Sie sind deutsch?*"

"*Ich war Lehrerin bei einer Frauenuniversität. Ich habe Deutsch unterrichtet. Auch Französisch.*"

"*Ach, es ist gut, die Muttersprache zu hören.*" Wilhelma nodded with obvious satisfaction. "*Hier gibt es keine anderen Deutsche.*"

"You two want to say somethin' in English so I can get in on the conversation?"

The ladies laughed at Virginia's complaint and leaned back as the kitchen crew stepped in and filled their water glasses. Shortly after, baskets of bread, bowls of mashed potatoes, and other side dishes made their way up and down the table, accompanied by the trays of chicken. Cecelia picked up a steaming, golden brown thigh and sniffed it. Immediately, her stomach growled. "I didn't realize I was so hungry." But then again, she hadn't eaten anything since dinner last night before getting on the train.

She picked up her knife and fork and started to cut the meat, but Virginia laid a hand atop hers. "We have to wait."

"For?"

"Miss Sally always says grace."

"Oh." As Cecelia laid her silverware back down, Miss Sally entered the room, and the buzz of the dozens of chattering women faded to silence almost immediately.

"I'm sorry I'm late," Miss Sally said, striding toward the open seat across from Cecelia. "And I know you're all starving. If you'd bow your heads for grace." Cecelia watched the heads drop and then followed suit. Miss Sally cleared her throat. "Oh, Beloved Father, thank You once again for the blessing of gathering with these lovely ladies to break bread and to fellowship. We thank You for Your provision, we praise You for Your steadfast love, and we glorify Your name in this place. Thank You for Your grace and what You did, Jesus, on the cross. May we never take You for granted. Amen."

Everyone commenced to eating, but Cecelia dug in a little more slowly now. She glanced around at the faces, some seemed to glow, some held tension in their expressions, some looked oblivious to everything but food. Did they all have a hurt in their past?

Was this about shoving religion on them, pressuring them to convert? *What is this place?* she wondered.

"Wondering what you've gotten yourself into?" Miss Sally asked as she filled her plate.

Cecelia blinked, surprised by the precision of the question, and cut into the chicken to avoid looking at the woman. "Maybe."

"Don't worry," Virginia said, elbowing her gently. "You get out of this what you put into it."

"Yes," Miss Sally said, pausing her fork in midair. "That's a wonderful way to put it, Virginia." She shifted her gaze to Cecelia. "You will leave here better off than when you came. But my prayer is you'll leave richer than you can imagine. It really is up to you."

Cecelia nodded, but the motion transformed into a shaking of her head. "I still don't think I understand."

"Don't vorry. You vill." Wilhelma plucked a piece of chicken from the tray in front of her, then another and another. "For now, start by enjoying the food and the company."

Yes, Cecelia would enjoy the food. And she wouldn't be rude to the people around her, but she had, in truth, no desire to draw close to any of them. Once this ordeal was over, or whatever one might call the time spent at Burning Dress, Cecelia would never see any of these women again, and the cowboy with those piercing, blue eyes would be a misty memory.

She didn't know where she would wind up, but she was thoroughly intent on distancing herself from people. And the pain they could inflict.

MISS SALLY TAPPED a spoon on her water glass as she rose to address the group. Cecelia laid her fork down, curious to hear. Anything that would give some insight to Burning Dress was welcome.

"Ladies, you are about to finish up, so I'd like to make an announcement. You've probably already smelled the smoke. We will be having a bonfire tonight."

A collective gasp practically sucked the air out of the room. It was followed instantly by eager cheers and applause. Miss Sally smiled at her group, but motioned for quiet. "Many of you know, I'm sure, Tallulah has expressed her desire to move on with her life."

Again, more cheers and applause rose. The ladies sitting closest to Tallulah hugged her and squeezed her shoulder. Cecelia was completely lost.

"I'll see you all at the fire in ten minutes." Miss Sally did not sit back down. Nodding at her table-mates, she disappeared through the kitchen.

Cecelia leaned over to Virginia. "What's going on?"

"Come watch, and then if you have any questions, I'll see if I can answer them."

AFTER DINNER, all the ladies—*only* ladies, noted Cecelia—gathered before a large, crackling fire outside. Miss Sally and Tallulah stood side-by-side facing the crowd.

"Most of you know Tallulah. When she came to us a year ago, she would barely speak or look you in the eye, much less offer friendship. Now, I'm happy to say she has recovered from the blow dealt her by her husband. The love of Jesus fills her heart. She is ready to live and love again.

"And to forgive. As she has been forgiven. To that end, she is letting go of her pain and her hurt. Tallulah." Miss Sally stepped aside, allowing Tallulah center stage.

Cecelia didn't understand. Virginia leaned over to her. "Tallulah's husband had an affair with her sister. They were all three servants in a wealthy man's home up in Boston—"

Tallulah produced a dress from behind her back. *A wedding gown?* Cecelia wondered. Made simply, but elegantly, of ivory satin and lace, Tallulah looked at it tenderly for a moment, drifting her fingers across the bodice, remembering days of hope and dreams?

"When I came here," she began, "I was clinging hard to a grudge. Hadn't talked to my husband, hadn't talked to my sister in three years. But I sure thought about 'em every day. The thoughts weren't none too kind, either. They were dark and spiteful thoughts that went on and on. The hate was eatin' me up. Lord, I was frail, bent over, miserable…and I reckon desperate. Which is why I came here."

"My," Cecelia whispered. *Look at her now...vibrant, healthy, lean, and strong.*

"The day Miss Sally led me to the Lord, everything started changing for me. I've written letters forgiving those who done me wrong. And I ain't gonna worry no more about what harm was done to me as an earthly bride. Tonight, all I'm worried about is being the bride of Christ."

With that, the woman turned and tossed the beautiful gown into the fire. Cecelia gasped. Cheers and applause went up as the dress erupted into flames and was quickly consumed. She crossed her arms, wondering at what she'd just seen, hanging back as the group rushed to embrace Tallulah and wish her well.

Cecelia overheard snatches of the conversations. The words *forgiven, saved, joyous,* and *hopeful* came up over and over. Tallulah was only looking forward now. Then Cecelia learned the woman was going to work at a mission in New Mexico, building and repairing homes for the local Indians. From a maid to a missionary. An unusual transition for anyone, but especially for a black woman in 1889.

Cecelia couldn't even begin to understand the transformation and decided she wouldn't try. After all, she was rather above it. She didn't hate her husband. She had come to terms with the fact that no love lasts. And everyone lies or says cruel things. Hence, life is safer when lived from a distance.

Still, she hoped Tallulah would be happy. As happy as anyone willing to give her life to serve others could be. The plan seemed an exercise in futility to Cecelia, but it wasn't her life.

CHAPTER THREE

DAWN HAD BARELY STREAKED THE SKY WITH A tangerine glow when Cecelia trudged out to the corral, stretching and yawning. She'd been told the hands would meet here to determine their tasks for the day. She discovered two young girls, late teens or maybe in their early twenties, trying futilely to get a blanket on an antsy, grumbling palomino whose lead line dangled from the halter.

"She wasn't like this yesterday," a chubby, Hispanic girl whined, lowering the blanket in her hands.

The other one, taller, a red braid trailing down her back, half-raised her hands, patting the air in an attempt to stop the horse's pacing. "What's gotten into you?"

Cecelia didn't know the horse well enough to guess at the underlying cause. It was pretty obvious, however, that the frustration mounting in the two humans was spilling onto the animal. "Horses are sensitive," she said amicably. "They can tell when you're getting frustrated with them, and they don't understand it. It confuses them."

The two hands looked at her sideways. "You an expert horsewoman?" The tall one asked, her gaze and tone as fiery as her hair.

Cecelia pursed her lips. "I don't mean to offend. It's just that if you two would step back, take a breath, she'd calm down. A little, at least."

"She's right." Miss Sally stepped up to the fence beside Cecelia, rested a hand on the top rail. "Molly, I can feel your frustration all the way out here."

Molly whipped off her hat, revealing more ruby hair, and slapped the Stetson against her thigh. "Jax said to be ready by 6:30. We're running behind because of this ornery critter."

"That's not the horse's fault. You know the rules. Treat everyone, even the animals—with dig—"

"With dignity and respect," the girl finished for her. Sighing heavily, she dropped the hat back over her head. "Yes, ma'am. We let ourselves get a little flustered."

The other girl hugged the saddle blanket to her chest and dropped her gaze.

"No harm done." Miss Sally slipped through the fence and approached the horse but stopped about fifteen feet from her. "Give me a minute with her." Shrugging, the two girls walked away to lean back on the fence.

Cecelia assumed Miss Sally might grab the lead line and attempt to work with the horse. Instead, she took two bold strides toward the animal but stopped when it looked like the horse might bolt. The pair stared at each other for a moment. The horse's ears twitched in every direction, but finally settled on the newest human in the corral.

Miss Sally smiled. "Now, let's you and I have a talk." She took one step toward the horse. A moment later, the horse took a step toward her. Sensing the tension had broken, Cecelia watched as Miss Sally, talking in low, but animated tones, approached the animal. Cecelia strained to hear, inclining an ear as Miss Sally touched the horse's cheek. The boss woman was whispering, moving her head, and motioning calmly with her hands, as if she were engaged in conversation with a human. At one point, she gestured toward the two hands. The horse grumbled. Miss Sally dropped her hands on her hips as if disapproving of something. The horse grumbled again, but Cecelia would have sworn it sounded... friendlier.

And Miss Sally's hands left her hips. She patted the horse on the right cheek and turned toward the two girls. "She'll be all right now, but you two quit double-teaming her. Maria"—the Hispanic girl's head snapped up—"your shorter stature doesn't make her as nervous as Molly's does. You'll ride Buttercup here today."

The girl sucked in a breath and straightened her hat. "Uh, *sí*, but Jax said she needs a more experienced rider. Especially first thing."

"You'll be fine. Molly, go get Leo, and while you're at it, bring out Twister for Cecelia."

Cecelia frowned. *Twister* didn't exactly sound like a friendly name for a horse. Molly nodded without betraying her thoughts on this plan and double-timed it to the barn.

Miss Sally glanced over at Cecelia, but then her gaze shot past her. "Mornin', Jax."

The man startled Cecelia with his silent approach. "Mornin', Miss Sally." He stopped beside her, pushing his hat back a touch. "Maria." He offered a slower, half-smile to Cecelia. "Cecelia."

She once again blinked at the stunning brilliance of the foreman's blue eyes. "Good morning."

Miss Sally joined them at the fence. "Jax, I took Molly off Buttercup here. She preferred to have Maria as her rider."

"All right. We'll put Molly on Leo then, and Cecelia here on...Twister?"

"That was my thought. Molly'll be out with them both in just a minute. And if Leo is fussy, switch him with Twister. But Leo usually prefers redheads."

"And Twister likes the new hands because he can show off," Jax said, winking at Cecelia.

Miss Sally laughed. "Exactly. He'll show Cecelia there how to do her job."

Jax joined in her laughter. "He does like pretending to be the boss."

This exchange befuddled Cecelia and she tugged on her ear in consternation. They spoke about these horses as if they could chat with them and get their thoughts on the day's chores. Then again, maybe they could. Cecelia had never seen anyone calm a horse just by talking to it.

Apparently, the expression on her face amused Miss Sally and the woman laughed harder. "I have a special way with our stock, Cecelia. You'll get used to it."

"All right." A nonsensical comment, but she didn't know what to say. Not much choice in the matter, anyway.

Miss Sally slipped back through the fence and nodded at Jax and Cecelia. "I'll see y'all at supper this evening, Lord willing."

"Yes, ma'am." Jax touched the brim of his hat as she passed. "Lookin' forward to it."

Excitement had crept into his voice, and Cecelia was intrigued. She waited a moment to talk, pleased to watch Maria saddle Buttercup without a hint of a problem. "What's going on for supper tonight?" she finally asked. *Another dress to burn, this time, the men get to watch?*

"It's Friday night. All the hands mix together for supper and play some cards or chess. Maybe do a little dancing. It breaks the monotony." Cecelia nodded, not inclined to look forward to any extra socializing, and knew she'd head off to bed early. Jax slapped the top rail, punctuating the end of chatting and the start of their chores. "All right, let's get moving. We're rotating pastures today."

ONCE JAX and the girls were in the saddle, they headed off toward the west. Cecelia introduced herself to Molly and Maria. The initial tension gone now that they were mounted, the girls were far more relaxed and friendly. Beyond the basic niceties, however, Cecelia preferred to admire the Wyoming countryside—rolling hills as green as fabled Ireland, a backdrop of jagged, blue mountains in the distance. She could stare at them for hours and, therefore, forced her attention back to the herd up on the hill.

"You don't talk much," Jax offered blandly, as he rode up beside her.

Cecelia almost grunted her agreement to prove him right when a thought crossed her mind. She motioned with her head to the pair of riders behind them. "These two are kind of young and don't seem to have a lot of experience. Are we all you've got?" She shrugged a shoulder. "Miss Sally talked like this place produced top hands."

"It does. And you and these two here are gonna mix in with a seasoned crew. They've been out here since dawn."

"Oh. We're new, so we got to sleep in?"

"Somethin' like that."

"Is everything Miss Sally said true, then? About Burning Dress turning out—"

"The best hands in the country. Bar none."

"Really?" Cecelia was eager to see evidence of it. She glanced back at Molly and Maria. Hard to believe those two would give a cowboy a run for his money.

"I'll tell ya somethin' else." Jax's voice was light and breezy, amusement obvious in his tone.

"And what's that?"

"This is the biggest ranch in the territory, and seventy-five percent of the employees are female, from the chuck wagon cook to most of the cowboys, to the goat wrangler."

"Biggest, meaning most successful?" She asked carefully, unsure if he was playing word games with her, since the two didn't necessarily mean the same thing.

A sideways grin highlighted a dimple in his left cheek. He looked over at her through long, dark lashes, his sapphire eyes flashing. "Most successful. Every ranch in the territory wants to be us." He shook his head, and the humor faded. "Doesn't sit too well with some of our neighbors."

"They don't like being bested by a mostly female ranch, huh?"

"No, they surely do not."

Cecelia couldn't stop the grin that appeared on her own lips. *Maybe I won't be so useless to womanhood after all, William.*

JAX COULD SEE Lowdy's crew on the next ridge, a half-mile out to the north. To his right, a little farther to the south, he caught sight of a dust cloud. Bar T boys. Bringing their herd as close to the property line as they could get—again.

Nothin' wrong with using every inch of your own land. Only, they had a tendency to cross onto Miss Sally's.

It annoyed him how Quitman and all the men over at the Bar T thought themselves so superior to everyone on the Burning Dress. Yet, this ranch was out-producing them almost two-to-one. And that fact was one big burr in Quitman Taylor's saddle.

"Jealous," he whispered. "Pea-green with it."

"Pardon?" Cecelia said from beside him, tracking his gaze.

He swished his reins back and forth. "We're bordered by the Bar T. They think they're special and entitled to some of Miss Sally's grass when the notion strikes."

"That's their dust?"

"Yep." He looked at her then, and tried to ignore her alluring, jade eyes that studied things with the aloofness of a cat. Admittedly, they tripped him up some. Because they struck him as familiar.

"Ever have any trouble with them?" she asked.

"Not so far." *But Taylor is pushing the edge.* Jax nudged his horse and rode up alongside Maria and Molly. "We're meeting up with Lowdy down at the creek. You two doin' all right on those mounts?" Both girls nodded. "All right, well, heads up. You're on drag for another few days." Disappointment streaked across their faces. "Not the most fun place, I know," he acknowledged, "but the safest. Those horses work out better for ya, I'll move ya." Out of the corner of his eyes, he saw the curious quirk in Cecelia's brow and told her, "You're most likely on left flank. You and one of the more experienced riders from Lowdy's crew." She nodded, in apparent acceptance.

As they headed toward the creek, Jax spotted Lowdy's crew doing the same, only driving a small herd of cattle before them. They all met at the bottom. Jax raised a hand in greeting at the lead cowboy, a muscular man of about forty. He had snow-white hair that made him look much older, and one of the twangiest, most nasally Texas accents Jax had ever heard. It always made him smile.

"Lowdy, mornin'." Jax had to speak up to be heard over the mooing, bellowing cattle splashing through the creek.

"Jax." Lowdy left his crew of six—four women, and two men—and trotted up. He scanned Maria, Molly, and then Cecelia with mild interest. "Got a new one, huh?"

"Yeah, this is Cecelia Huggins."

He nudged his horse forward to shake her hand. "Cecelia. Nice to know ya."

"And you."

"You ride?"

"Some."

"She's one of the better ones we've had so far," Jax told him. Her surprised look said she hadn't expected the compliment. He only spoke the truth. "And Maria and Molly are coming right along," he added, attempting to keep the girls' confidence up.

"Hmmm." Lowdy *tsked* as if he wasn't sure of the claim, but shrugged. "Well, let's get a move on then.

'Celia, ride with me. We're taking left flank." As she rode toward the new boss, Lowdy looked at Jax. "You stayin' or heading back?"

"Heading back unless you need me."

"Nah." He squinted at Cecelia. "Reckon if you say she'll do, she'll do."

Confident the women were all on good mounts and in good hands, Jax tipped his hat to the ladies and turned his horse back to Burning Dress. Cecelia's piercing gaze stayed with him, though, as he bounded over the prairie, dredging up unwanted memories. Memories of another woman with eyes as green as oriental jade. A woman who had lied to him as easily as a healthy man takes a breath.

He kicked his horse, Nickels, up into an easy lope and let the animal's rhythm, the wind in his face, the freedom of these open hills, put the painful recollections to bed, for a spell. Life had kicked him in the gut. Just as it had the women at the ranch. They were all recovering from some hurt or abuse, he gathered. The last thing in the world they or Jax wanted was any romantic complications. The other male ranch hands were good, steady men who had eyes only for their wives. Personally, Jax was happy to wind up a confirmed bachelor. In fact, he was the first single cowboy Miss Sally had ever hired.

He could see the genius, now, in why she had put certain people in certain places or had hired certain kinds of men. She knew everyone's history. She'd told Jax the women were to work and not be chased or flirted with in any way.

She'd sure picked a winner with him. Love, for Jax, was like mixing oil and water. He'd tried it. The result had torn his heart from his chest. He would never, ever risk it again. He was the perfect man to be on a ranch surrounded by women, especially one with haunting, green eyes that reminded him why he was here in the first place.

AT SUNSET, Jax entered the barn to check on the girls, but paused in the entrance, perplexed by Cecelia's behavior. She had dismounted and stood facing her saddle. Her forehead rested on the seat jockey, her arms were draped limply over the horse, but she was completely still.

Is she asleep?

Twister waited patiently, not even swishing his tail, as if he understood the woman's exhaustion and could give her time to find her strength. Beyond Cecelia, the other girls were taking care of their horses, but with only a smidgen more energy.

Jax almost laughed at the oft-repeated image of a trail-weary hand but knew better. He'd come to understand women didn't have much of a sense of humor about things when they were asked to do a man's job. They interpreted the laughter as being at their expense when it was simply funny to see any new cowboy worn out, saddle sore, and nearly asleep on his feet. Jax would have called it an initiation into ranch work. And he thought Cecelia's turn at it made her…kind of, well, almost adorable.

Jax meandered up to her, thumbs hooked in his front pockets. "So, how'd you do on your first day?" Snuffing the humor in his voice took real effort.

Cecelia slowly raised her head. "I didn't think it was possible for my a—I mean, my rear end to hurt this much. I can't feel my arms. I swear I could sleep standing up."

Jax bit back the laughter, dragged a hand across his chin to hide the rebellious smile. "A bath and a meal always help." He tilted his head, puzzled. Cecelia still hadn't moved, and he frowned. "You want some help with your saddle?"

She did move then, to eye the other girls in the barn doing their work, and her chin came up. "No," she said with surprising firmness.

He didn't take offense at the curt answer. It said everything he needed to know. "All right then." He stepped back. "I'll see all you ladies at supper."

CECELIA GOT a second wind after dinner and determined to put in a brief appearance at the Friday night festivities. The large parlor was bustling with people and alive with rippling laughter when she entered. Wilhelma and Virginia were playing Old Maid off to her right and waved.

Two cowboys were playing dominoes with Molly and Maria at a table tucked in the corner near the fireplace. The men had been on Lowdy's crew today. The fella with the patch on his eye, a touch grizzled, probably in his thirties, was called Bug. Cecelia grinned. Not a name one forgot. The other man, maybe late twenties, wore his blond hair cropped short and had a forgettable face. And name. She bit down on her lip, thinking. Nope. Couldn't remember it. Both men were married, but their wives worked in town. The two females loitering not far from the cowboys, however, implied they had been invited to the festivities.

She surveyed the rest of the room as she drifted about absently. Two young ladies sat on the couch, reading quietly. Cecelia had seen them working in the garden. The dark-haired girl—Barbara, maybe?—bounced her leg as she flipped pages. A nervous tick? Like she couldn't wait to run from the room and smoke a cigarette...or take a drink. Cecelia wondered if alcohol was Barbara's personal demon. She glanced over the room. Wasn't the implication that they all had some demon they were here to fight? Some wound that had turned into a destructive force?

This perplexed Cecelia. She didn't feel as if she had any healing or demon-slaying to do. So why was she here? To free up Reverend Springer's basement?

Miss Sally was standing near the fireplace, smoking a cigar and talking to Maude. She was the only woman in the room still in pants. All the others had changed, yet even in dungarees, the boss lady still looked the most elegant. Just beyond them, Lowdy and Jax sat at a small table playing cards. Poker,

Cecelia guessed. Only, instead of chips, a pile of toothpicks rose between them.

"Come, join us, 'Celia." A hand grabbed for Cecelia, startling her back a step and bringing her hand to her chest. Virginia laughed, looking more surprised than normal. "Gads, you're jumpy as a squirrel." She motioned to the game she and Wilhelma were playing. "Git your heart outta your throat and come play Old Maid with us."

Without much enthusiasm, Cecelia nodded. "All right. Just one round, though. I'm going to bed early."

"You are pooped, *yah*?" Wilhelma asked, passing out the cards as they sat.

"*Yah*," Cecelia echoed.

"The first day is—how you say, worst? But it is a good kind of tired, *yah*?"

Cecelia thought about it for a moment. William hadn't crossed her mind once out on the range today, she'd been so busy trying to get used to riding again, following orders yelled at unfriendly volumes, and then the new challenge of chasing wandering steers, reading their directions—it had all occupied her mind, worn her body down. She sighed lightly and gathered up her cards. "Yes, I suppose it is."

"You enjoy the work of a cowboy?" Virginia asked, tossing a three of Clubs down.

"It brought back some good memories," Cecelia said without elaborating. Namely, memories of her childhood home, a farm outside Richmond.

"My pappy woulda made a good cowboy." Virginia sorted through her hand as she thought aloud. Her voice rose with admiration. “He could ride a horse in them Tennessee hollers like some kinda ghost. He was in the cavalry in the war. Never got shot once, but had three horses shot out from under him.”

Cecelia merely nodded and watched as Wilhelma laid down a six of Clubs.

“Why did you leave teaching?” The German girl asked, watching Cecelia over her cards.

“I never enjoyed it. I fell into it because my mother taught school. When I married, I quit.”

Though Virginia and Wilhelma did not know Cecelia’s history, the mention of marriage seemed to dampen the conversation. The three fell silent for a round.

Finally, Wilhelma started the talk again. “Marriage. I don’t know about you two, but it did not work so good for me.”

Cecelia rotated the stiffness from her neck. “Definitely left a little something to be desired for me, as well.”

Virginia’s face fell and she stared at her cards. Cecelia was surprised to see an expression on the girl that actually reflected sadness.

“My Bo was a good man,” she said as if to no one in particular. “He put up with a lot. I took to drinkin’ when I was fourteen.” She swallowed. “When it caused me to lose a child…he…well, he—”

Cecelia slid her hand over and touched Virginia’s forearm, stopping her story. “Don’t relive it. Let it be.” No good would come from sharing painful memories over a card game with women who were mostly strangers. Cecelia planned to heed this advice herself. Virginia nodded, and the game continued, though with a noticeably somber mood in the group.

After a few hands, however, Virginia shook her head. "You're right. We can't wallow in our heartbreaks like pigs in mud. Our lives ain't over. We've got livin' left to do, more joy coming."

"*Yah*, it is not good to hang on to the brokenness. What is it Miss Sally says? Laughter doeth a heart good."

"But a broken heart, who can stand?" Cecelia muttered softly, puzzled that she knew the scripture. But much about her life now, the Burning Dress, these women sitting here, puzzled her. She couldn't really explain why she was at this ranch, yet she felt it was no accident.

"Baxter's going to start up the fiddle," Miss Sally announced. "I say we do a little square dancing." Happy chirps and applause rose from the group. "Maude here has agreed to lend Lowdy to us as a dance partner, so with him and Jax, Bug, Baxter, and Dub, you ladies should get your share of dances in."

Cecelia cleared her head with a curt shake and laid down her cards. Dancing was the last thing she was in the mood to do, especially for some reason with Jax. "I'm sorry, ladies, please excuse me. I can barely keep my eyes open."

She didn't wait for any goodbyes, just nodded and rose from the table.

JAX WATCHED HER GO, wondering why she was cutting a path out of here like her skirt was on fire…

"Can we finish this hand 'fore the dancing starts?"

Lowdy's question brought him back to the game. "Sorry, let's see…" He studied the straight in his hand and pondered his wager.

"You taking a shine to the new girl?"

"No." The question cut through the distracted fog in Jax's head and he repeated his answer more firmly. "No. She just reminds me of somebody I'd rather forget." He placed three toothpicks on the pile. "I'll see your bet and raise you…" He added another pair. "Two picks."

"Them's the ones you got to worry about." Lowdy wiggled his eyebrows, white hair falling over his forehead. "The ones who *remind you* of somebody. Show's you have a type. Be careful, or you'll get sucked in again."

Before Jax could say anything, Maude stepped up and lovingly pushed the hair out of her husband's eyes. "You boys about done here? That fiddle is going to be calling my name, husband."

"I'm waiting on you, my princess." Lowdy winked at Jax, taking his wife's hand and squeezing it.

Jax took the cue. "I'm folding. You're too good for me, Lowdy. Take him on, Maude, before I don't have a toothpick to my name."

A mischievous grin bloomed on Lowdy's stubbly cheeks, and he pushed his worthless winnings into a pile with a wink. He rose, draped his arm around Maude, and directed his plump wife toward the space opening up in front of the hearth. As Baxter tuned his fiddle, Jax gathered up and tapped the cards into a neat stack. He couldn't help chuckling at the pair. They'd be happy with each other 'til their last breath.

The smile melted.

He envied them.

"How did Cecelia do today?"

Miss Sally's voice mercifully broke into his melancholy thoughts. He rose and joined her at the fire, dodging Baxter's bow. "She rides well. No exaggeration there. And Lowdy said she worked like ten men. Never took a break."

"No." Miss Sally tilted her head. "How is she doing?"

He shrugged. All he could offer was a subjective observation. "She keeps to herself and has a shell around her."

"Yes." Miss Sally drummed her fingers on the glass of punch in her hands. "Remains to be seen, I guess, if it's a turtle shell or an eggshell."

If Jax had to guess, he would have put his money on the turtle shell.

CHAPTER FOUR

Cecelia slept fitfully until the wee hours of the morning. Around her in the dark, unfamiliar surroundings, she could hear the soft, delicate breaths of the other women. Too soft to drown out her own thoughts. Her mind stubbornly wandered back to William's brutal insults echoing over and over in the quiet. She squeezed her eyes shut, trying to close out the loathsome words, but they were in her. Part of her now.

Sighing, she sat up and tossed the quilt off her legs.

Uncannily bright moonlight streamed in the windows on either side of the fireplace and through the four dormers in the room. She thought perhaps a stealthy trip to the kitchen for a bite of cheese or a boiled egg might settle her tumultuous mind. She tugged on her robe and slipped out of the room.

She was tiptoeing down the stairs when she thought she heard a sniffle and stopped. She waited to see if the sound would repeat itself. A moment later, she heard it again. Someone crying? Moving slowly to silence the soft rustle of her gown, she inched down the open-tread stairs. A gentle flutter of a curtain drew her eyes to the back porch at the end of the main hall. The French door was open, and she heard the sniffle again.

Cecelia didn't want to intrude, but just in case someone was in need, she crept down the hall, giving a nervous glance to an eerily shadowed bear's head on the wall. At the door, she rested a hand on the frame and peered outside. On the stone veranda, populated with ferns and empty rocking chairs, Virginia sat alone, staring forlornly at a rag doll in her lap. She caressed the little toy's face and sniffled again. Suddenly, as if a dam broke, a sob tore free, and Virginia crushed the doll to her breast. Her shoulders shook violently with her weeping.

Cecelia placed a hand over her mouth. Memories of her own nights like this flooded back. A tight knot swelled in her chest, and tears pooled in her eyes.

"Oh, forgive me," Virginia pleaded into the doll. "Please, forgive me." Her voice dropped to a choked whisper. "I hate myself so much. So much."

Unexpectedly moved by Virginia's pain, Cecelia had to turn away. She couldn't imagine losing a child, especially since she'd wanted a baby to hold so badly. Virginia's pain had to be unimaginable.

Swallowing the lump in her throat, Cecelia headed back upstairs. Though now her steps, still quiet, were weary and sad. She would lie down again.

But she would not sleep.

CHAPTER FIVE

SATURDAY ON THE BURNING DRESS HAD A SLIGHTLY different feel to it. Maybe because instead of moving cattle, Cecelia was assigned to assist Virginia in cleaning, checking, and repairing tack. The girl's eyes were rimmed with red, but she seemed mostly to have dealt with her midnight bout of grief.

Glad for that and happy with the little change of pace, Cecelia set up a table outside the barn to take advantage of the warm day and started by laying all the available halters on it. She planned to inspect them carefully, clean them, and pass off to Virginia any in need of repair.

She was pouring neatsfoot oil into a bowl when half a dozen girls burst from the main house. Giggling, laughing, and holding the hems of their freshly laundered dresses out of the dirt, they hurried toward the barn.

"What's the occasion?" Cecelia asked, spotting Wilhelma in the group.

"It is Saturday," she said carefully through her accent. "Miss Sally goes to town and takes whoever wants to go."

Cecelia frowned. No one had told her of this trip. She wouldn't have minded going, getting off the ranch, picking up a few things. She certainly had a craving for some black licorice.

"Oh, I misspeak," Wilhelma corrected. "She takes whoever wants to go who can. New girls aren't allowed until they've been on the ranch for a month."

"Why?"

Virginia came out of the barn then, a set of reins in her hand. "I think it's because she wants to make sure you've got your feet 'neath ya before ya hear the gossip. The town thinks we're out here doing voodoo or some such mess." The group of women with Wilhelma quieted down, lowered their gazes as if they'd been personally accused of something dark and lascivious. "Don't pay those folks no never mind," she urged the girls. "They say stupid things. Like, Miss Sally's a witch doctor or a medicine woman."

"That's ludicrous," Cecelia said.

"That mean *shtupid*?" Wilhelma asked.

She nodded. "*Yah*."

"It is *shtupid* then."

Molly took a step forward. Cecelia almost didn't recognize the girl in a dress and without her cowboy hat. She lifted her chin indignantly, resting a hand on her hip. "We're a mostly female-run ranch that does better than two-thirds of the outfits in these parts. That makes folks wanna gossip."

Virginia jangled the reins in her hand, her eyes frosting over. "We don't talk about what goes on out here because some of u—I mean, some of these girls are running from husbands who would just as soon shoot 'em as look at 'em." She brought her attention back to the group. "But the secrecy leaves room for tall tales."

For the second time since Cecilia had met her, the happy-surprised expression on Virginia's face clouded. It disturbed Cecelia. The girl wasn't meant to be downcast. "Say, if I give one of you girls a nickel, will you bring me some licorice?" She was surprised at herself for trying to break the tension, but Virginia snapped back to the moment and her countenance lightened again.

"Oh, *yah*." Wilhelma extended her hand. "Happy to."

"Me, too." Virginia fished in her front pocket and produced a coin. "Here's a dime. I'm buying 'Celia's."

"You don't have—"

"You get it next time."

Something in the girl's smile convinced Cecelia to accept the gesture. "All right. Next time."

JAX TUGGED his hat a touch lower as he and his horse, Nickels, rode past the only saloon in Hell's Half-Acre. A pretty brunette in a form-fitting, midnight blue gown leaned against a post and winked at him. He ignored the obvious invitation and kept riding. The closest thing to a town near Burning Dress was this rough-and-tumble settlement with the unholy name. One thousand, one hundred and twenty souls resided in its weathered limits, and most all of them were in some way beholden to the town founder, an Englishman named Sam Hain.

Jax didn't think much of Hain. He didn't think much of any man who kept women around for the purpose of selling their bodies. But Hain also puzzled him. He owned the saloon, the hotel, the mercantile, and the bank, but Hell's Half-Acre wasn't exactly Denver. Yet, the man was rolling in money. And power. Was that why he stayed in this backwoods village?

He lorded his wealth and his economic stranglehold of the town over everyone in it. Nobody crossed him. Nobody gave him any trouble. Not without penalty. Jax had seen him lose his temper a time or two at the saloon. Hain gave no quarter, mercilessly making examples of any offending parties. In a town without a badge, he could get away with it.

Even Jax's own father had said you might cross a lot of men, but Hain shouldn't be one of them.

If any other area of commerce had been closer, Jax would have made the effort to shop there. Twenty miles over to Riverton, though, was just a little too far when he needed mundane things like soap and a razor. Besides, Miss Sally had negotiated special rates with Hain.

Accepting things as they were for the time being, Jax rode up to the hitching post in front of the mercantile and dismounted. He didn't need much, but this freshly white-washed, well-stocked store was the place to get it.

Surprisingly, he found the mercantile quiet and empty of customers. He assumed Ned, the clerk, must be in the back. Being about his own business, Jax headed toward the toiletries, but on a whim strode to the far corner. He had a shirt in need of buttons and chose to peruse the selection. Maybe one of the gals back at the ranch would be kind enough to sew them on for him. Maybe Cecelia would do him the favor.

He chided himself for the thought. He didn't know her that well. Maybe Virginia then—

The bell over the door chimed and he looked up just as motion at the counter caught his eye. Sam Hain stepped out from the back room, a ledger in his hands, but his gaze was trained on the door. From his position, Jax couldn't make out who had just entered.

"Good morning, Sally." Hain greeted the woman with his polished, proper inflection. It sounded as refined as English tea, but Jax knew in an instant it could turn to unnerving cold steel.

Miss Sally strode up to Hain with the swagger no one else in town dared to use. "Got a bone to pick with you, Sam."

Hain was a devilishly handsome, well-dressed man in his fifties with wavy, jet-black hair that didn't allow a speck of gray, and a meticulously trimmed beard that looked as if the barber visited him daily. Unless annoyed, he was soft-spoken and quite genteel, and

Jax wondered which way Miss Sally's tone would push him.

Hain sighed, presumably at Miss Sally's warning, but not before Jax caught the flash of tenderness that passed over the man's face. Only it disappeared so fast, Jax wondered if he'd imagined it.

"Whatever is the matter?" he asked, a bored expression playing on his face as he laid the ledger down. "The flour I sold you ground too fine?" He opened the book and began casually perusing the pages, dragging his finger down the columns, ignoring her.

No one ignored Miss Sally.

She splayed her hand on the ledger and leaned in. Hain looked up, and their eyes locked. "You need to tell your supplier that the last batch of barbed wire was sorry. We had a devil of a time stringing it without breaking it." Hain's face hardened, but Miss Sally pushed on. "Tell him it's defective or you need to price it according to what it really is: chicken wire."

Hain pulled the ledger away from her and slammed it shut. Straightening to his full height, an easy six-foot-six, he hung a thumb in his watch pocket and lifted an eyebrow at the woman. "There's nothing wrong with the wire."

Their fuss was interrupted by another customer entering the store. Quitman Taylor paused at the door and surveyed the two people at the counter. *The other big man in town,* Jax thought sourly, and backed out of sight as Taylor strode toward Miss Sally and Hain.

He was also a tall man, solidly built, but about

twenty years older than Hain, with salt-and-pepper hair he wore cut close. He casually plucked a pickle from the barrel and took a juicy bite as he joined the pair at the counter. "Could be, Miss Sally, your ladies just don't know how to handle wire. Maybe they're more suited to an older profession." He winked amicably at Hain, as if the two were best friends, and pulled a handkerchief from his pocket to wipe his chin. "That's the rumor."

Miss Sally frowned at the man like he was a petulant middle-schooler. Hain, on the other hand, glared. "Keep comments like that to yourself, Taylor," he growled.

The rancher's eyes widened, as if taken aback by Hain's unfriendly response. Curling a lip, he straightened up. "You mean save 'em for when I visit your girls?"

Hain came from behind the counter. Gently but firmly pushing Miss Sally out of the way, he stepped up to Taylor, extending a clear challenge. His raised chin, the cold look in his eyes reminded Jax of a snake uncoiling, moving to within striking distance.

"I mean when you address Miss Sally, you will talk to her like the ang—*lady* she is. Do I make myself clear?"

Taylor studied Hain's face, tried to maintain an air of bravado, but under the other man's burning gaze, abandoned it after a moment with a nod and stepped back. "My apologies, Miss Sally." He sounded rattled, surprising Jax. "I didn't mean to offend."

"Yes, you did, but I don't care," she fired back

blandly. "You're a pitiful soul, Taylor. I know you're spending Saturday nights at Sam's Place and Sunday mornings in God's House. A man of your age shouldn't be talking to the Lord out both sides of his mouth."

"'Tis true," Hain said thoughtfully, wilting a little. "God will not be mocked."

The man's tone, a mix of awe and disdain, fascinated Jax. He sounded like a man with firsthand knowledge. This whole exchange, in fact, reeked of intimate history, deep relationships—perhaps broken ones—and inexplicable alliances.

"Salvation is yours for the asking, Quitman." Miss Sally's voice was gentle, but full of passion, even sympathy. "Don't be foolish and ignore Him. You're not going to live forever."

Taylor moved away from them both, his gaze ricocheting from Miss Sally to Hain, then back to her. "You two are crazy." He snorted in disgust, wheeled around, and charged for the exit, waving the pickle overhead. "I'll come back when the sermon's over."

The door shut with a loud thud, and an awkward silence settled on the store. Jax should have made his presence known, but he was fascinated by the mysterious dance going on here between the lady rancher and Hain.

Miss Sally looked at the town lord, her brow furrowed with regret, or pity. "I could say the same thing to you."

"What, that I'm crazy?"

"No. Talking out both sides of your mouth."

"I'm not mocking God. You of all people should know that. Yet, here I am reaping what I've sown."

"His mercies are new every day. You can always still ask—"

"I'm way past forgiveness, Sally." Hain clenched his teeth together and took a breath, as if working to calm himself. "Some people don't want redemption." He motioned around him, anger seeping into his voice as he spoke. "So, I'll stay here and rule in my little corner of hell." Miss Sally dropped her gaze as if the words were a slap. Suddenly, Hain slammed his fist down on the counter. "Tell me why I'm here. Why didn't I go with the others?"

She didn't flinch, nor did she look up. "How many times are you going to ask me that?"

"Until you answer me."

"I told you. Because He's merciful."

"This isn't mercy," he hissed. He inched toward her, entwined his gaze with hers. "It's the worst kind of torture." His anger was unmistakable, but Jax saw something else there, too. Something more vulnerable. Miss Sally faced the man's burning stare with her own gentle look. Finally, Hain shook his head. "I'm lost, Sally. The darkness in me—"

"Doesn't have to win."

He chuckled, a cold, bitter sound. "You should learn to accept defeat."

"You know that's impossible for me."

Hain's lips twitched over a clamped jaw, as if he was holding back a barrage of words, but then he growled and stormed from the store. Watching him go, Jax thought at that instant he'd give a hundred dollars and his best horse to know the story between these two.

He immediately regretted the selfish thought. Miss Sally's pained expression showed she was grieving over something having to do with this man. Jax felt worse for the eavesdropping. She sniffled and appeared to blink back tears. Filled with compassion for her and ashamed of himself, he removed his hat and raked a hand through his hair, wondering how he could make his presence known—

"Jax, you don't have to hide." He nearly jumped out of his skin as Miss Sally sighed and looked heavenward. "But I would appreciate your discretion."

He cleared his throat and stepped out into the aisle. "Of course." He joined her at the counter and laid down his buttons. "I didn't mean—"

"It's all right," she whispered, then turned toward the back of the store and yelled, "Ned, are you waiting on customers today or shall we help ourselves to what we need?"

Jax glanced at the door. He had a pretty strong suspicion Sam Hain wouldn't mind if she did.

Not at all.

On the other hand, he doubted Taylor would be extended the same courtesy. Or anybody else in town, for that matter.

CECELIA PULLED a harness from the bowl of oil, let it drip for a moment, then laid it on the table with at least a dozen halters she had already cleaned. Twenty feet away, Virginia sat on the front porch of the leather shop, stitching awl in hand, running catgut through leather and sewing it around the skeleton of a stirrup. The warm, early summer sunshine had been too welcoming to pass up, and they'd been out in it for a few hours now. Cecelia could feel her nose turning pink. "I'll need to get my hat soon, I think."

"Yeah, much more of this and we'll both freckle like an old possum."

Cecelia bit down a smile. "And that sounds bad."

"Ain't purty." She grunted with the effort of working with the taut leather. "This one's a booger, but I'll get it."

The ranch was quiet. Cecelia listened purposefully for a moment as she wiped the harness down. The ever-present sound of cattle was faint but there. Out in what they called the Big Box, a pasture of thirty-four acres, the ranch's horses grazed languidly, nickering and whinnying now and then. A rooster crowed behind the barn. A goat bleated.

Unfortunately, she could also hear William's voice whispering in her head when it was quiet like this. His vicious, heartless attacks echoed back and forth in the canyons of her mind. Sometimes, he sounded so close, so real, she turned, expecting to see him.

"You shame womanhood. What an utter failure you are." "You contribute nothing to this marriage. Worse for

you, no one else will want you now, either." "You don't seriously think I will continue to take care of you?"

Yes, I did think that. It was in our vows, you pompous, self-righteous peacock.

Cecelia took a deep breath and straightened up. "Enough," she whispered. "Life goes on. Go with it and forget him."

"You're muttering." Virginia shifted on the porch, repositioning the stirrup and the stitching awl. "You thinkin' about the husband?"

"He pops into my head now and then. But I'm getting better."

"You wanna talk about it?"

"No." She realized that sounded curt. Virginia was simply being Virginia. "No...but thank you for asking."

"Sure." The girl bowed her head and went back to work.

Cecelia felt like a callous fool for working so hard to keep Virginia at a distance. She was grieving and deserved some kindness. After all, Cecelia had had a few of her own instances of gut-wrenching sobs. Never had she felt more alone in those moments.

Virginia was putting on a brave face today, but Cecelia could see the pain behind the mask. She scolded herself for noticing. Scolded herself even more for caring.

This internal struggle was proof that she was getting too close. She hated it. She didn't want any friends here. She didn't want to care. And, yet, a question burst forth from her mouth: "You're all right today?"

A few more minutes of industrious silence passed before the girl answered. "I ain't all right, but I guess I'm not all wrong, either."

Cecelia nodded. "I think I know what you mean. We're entitled to some off days."

"It's just that healing is hard and, yeah, some days I do better than others."

"I'm sure losing a child is unimaginably painful. You need to give yourself time. Plenty of time."

"I reckon."

"How long have you been here?"

Virginia glanced up at the blue sky, as if the answer were there in the clouds. "Right at three months now."

More time slipped by in companionable silence as they washed, scrubbed, oiled, cut pieces of leather, sewed, and punched. Cecelia made an effort to locate hardware in the tack room and do some small repairs herself on the halters. When she came outside again, Virginia was working quietly. Her countenance was troubled, as if her thoughts had drifted back to dark memories, and it bothered Cecelia to see the girl downcast. It was unnatural for one so naturally chipper.

She wished she knew something to brighten the girl up a bit, but at the same time, desperately wished not to entangle herself. Yet, the loss of a child—how utterly heartbreaking. It tugged at her own heart. If

Cecelia could have only had a baby, she would have been so happy.

"How many children do you have?" she heard herself ask, as if her mouth had a mind of its own. Why couldn't she stop reaching out to this girl?

"Four. Two boys and two girls…I mean, two boys, one girl now." She faded off.

"The one you lost. How old was she? I'm sorry. If you don't want to ta—"

"Her name was Sadie. She was two years old. Had the fieriest red hair you ever saw, and it was always in a tangle of curls."

"Oh, I'm sure she was precious."

"You got no children?"

"No, and that's why my husband put me out. I can't have any. I didn't know until after I was married." Cecelia was surprised at letting the detail slip out—at this whole conversation—and quickly went back to scrubbing a halter.

"My Sadie was precious." Virginia's hands stilled.

Cecelia's slowed as she smiled at the woman's expression of bliss.

"We have a farm in the hills of Tennessee," she explained. "My little angel loved walking in the garden, digging her toes down into the dirt, watching the Woolly Worms crawl up the tree trunks… Last summer was so warm with just a little rain at night. We left the cabin door open all the time."

Cecelia bit her bottom lip. She didn't want to hear of the child, what, wandering off, getting lost in the woods?

"I'd tell you how I lost her. I'm afraid you won't like me very much, if I do, though." She stared down at her hands.

"Accidents happen, Virgin—"

"Weren't no accident."

Cecelia stilled herself. She sensed Virginia had something to say, some confession to make, so she remained quiet.

"I tipped the jug. The more I did, the more it got hold a me." Her face crumpled with grief. "I fell asleep, and little Sadie wandered out the door, down to the crik."

Cecelia flinched. *Oh, God, how awful...*

"Found her at sunset." Virginia's voice warbled with the pressure of strangled sobs. "I'll never forget the sight of all that red hair, glistening in the sun, floating in the water..." She dropped the items in her hands and covered her face. "My little girl's lifeless body." She wept quietly for a moment before Cecelia mustered the courage to go sit beside her. Instantly, Virginia collapsed on her.

Taken aback, out of her element with all this emotion, Cecelia managed to wrap the girl in an awkward hug, patting her shoulder. Yet, there had been a time when she'd given hugs freely. Cried with friends. Loved without fear. Didn't *expect* people to hurt her.

That Cecelia seemed to have lived a hundred years ago. Before William's eviscerating words had cut the heart out of her.

Or so she'd thought. Tears pooled unexpectedly in

her own eyes. "I'm so sorry, Virginia. I wish I could say something..." But she couldn't even begin to imagine the guilt and the grief the girl must war with every day. How would you ever get past it? Ever forgive yourself? Tragedies happened every day, but to be the cause of one that took the life of your child...

"Miss Sally"—the girl sniffled, but kept her face pressed to Cecelia's shoulder—"Miss Sally said the Lord knows my pain. He grieves with me. And He forgives me."

"I'm sure He does. I'm sure He does." And if this line of thinking helped Virginia heal, then Cecelia was all for it.

"She said if He could forgive Adam for bringing the curse of sin and death on the whole human race, He would forgive me, too." Virginia wiped her eyes and sat up. Cecelia quickly blinked her own tears away. "She made me memorize a verse of scripture. 'Ephesians. There is therefore now no condemnation for those who are in Christ Jesus.' He don't condemn me. She said I shouldn't, either." She sniffled and wiped her nose on the back of her hand. "I reckon maybe the hard part is forgiving myself. Don't know if I'll ever get there, but Miss Sally says Jesus loves me and He don't love junk."

Cecelia laced her fingers in her lap. She didn't know Jesus. Had no idea what He did or didn't like, but she liked hearing He loved Virginia.

Beside her, the girl offered a timid, sideways glance. "Sorry, I got your shirt all wet."

Cecelia shrugged off her concern. Virginia sniffed once more and picked up the stirrup and awl and began her work again. Cecelia started to rise but felt compelled to offer something more substantial than merely *I'm sure He does.* The woman was in pain and needed some compassion. Offering it wouldn't hitch Cecelia to her for life but might make her smile. "We're all human, Virginia. We all make mistakes. All of us. Miss Sally's right." She squeezed her shoulder. "I'm sure He does forgive you."

"Do you?" she asked in a rush. "Do you forgive me?"

"What?" The question confused Cecilia. The girl's hopeful gaze almost frightened her. "Why do you care what I think?"

Her gaze drifted off and her shoulders sagged. "I was just wonderin' how awful it sounds to somebody who don't know me well."

Cecelia thought about the question a moment and decided to try to answer it as honestly as she could. "I see your pain, Virginia. You're heartbroken." She struggled for the words to explain. Maybe she didn't even understand this herself. "You're suffering so deeply for a mistake. And the fact is, humans make mistakes. All of us." Cecelia felt bad for Virginia, which meant she had thus far failed to bury the spark of humanity in her soul, try as she might. "I hate to see you so undone by it. I guess the answer is yes, of course I could forgive you. I do forgive you." She shrugged a shoulder. "For what my forgiveness is worth."

Cecelia shrugged off the concern Virginia [illegible] once more and [illegible] by the [illegible] and [illegible] [illegible] Cecelia [illegible] [illegible] [illegible] [illegible] [illegible] [illegible] [illegible] [illegible] [illegible] [illegible] [illegible]

[illegible]

[illegible]

[illegible] who [illegible] [illegible]

[illegible] [illegible] [illegible] [illegible] [illegible] [illegible] [illegible] [illegible] [illegible] [illegible] [illegible] [illegible] [illegible] [illegible] mistakes. All [illegible] Cecelia [illegible] for Virginia [illegible] [illegible] [illegible] [illegible] [illegible] [illegible] [illegible] [illegible] would.

CHAPTER SIX

ROLLING A STIFF SHOULDER, JAX STOOD UP IN THE saddle and watched the herd grazing peacefully down in the draw. Only five hundred head here. In another few minutes, they'd start pushing them back toward Bare Bone's ridge and let them meander around in those wide, emerald canyons. Molly, Maria, and a string-bean of a girl named Helen were on the hill opposite. Somewhere, behind him, Cecelia was pushing strays toward the ravine.

Things in hand for the moment, he settled back into his saddle. For the umpteenth time, his thoughts drifted away to the discussion he'd witnessed between Miss Sally and Hain. It troubled him, though he couldn't say why. There wasn't a single person in town who had a kind word for the man. In fact, more than a few had whispered accusations of murder. But no bodies had been brought forth. Didn't mean Hain wasn't a killer. In fact, Jax leaned toward thinking he was. There was something dark and unpredictable about the man—like a short-tempered dog. And that dog had taken a liking to only one human. Miss Sally. But why her? It didn't seem…natural.

Behind him, a soft, sweet melody drifted to his ears, a feminine voice humming a song…one that struck a familiar chord. His heart hitched as he revisited a pretty girl with auburn hair, haunting green eyes, and a thick, French accent. The memory immediately brought a stab of pain. Good riddance to a liar and a cheat.

Cecelia rode up, still humming, but softer now. Jax acknowledged her with a slight tilt of his head. One minute, he could hurt over the pain Pauline had inflicted, and in the next, feel a little smile try to work free when he looked at Cecelia. That didn't make any sense at all. "Any strays?" he asked, working to keep his mind on his job.

"No, least not that I saw."

"That tune you were humming. I've heard it before. Used to know someone who sang it." So much for staying focused.

"It was fairly popular a few years back. *Où est mon coeur*, I believe is the name."

"Yeah, that's it. I never did know what she was singing about." Jax didn't miss the nervous way Cecelia turned her face away and her eyes darted around, as if she was trying to avoid a response. Which meant *she* knew what it was about. "Enlighten me?"

Cecelia scratched her nose with a dirty, gloved hand. "I'm not sure I know the whole story."

"Yes, you do."

They looked at each other, and he tried to communicate with an unblinking stare that he wanted the truth. Cecelia sighed and gazed off toward the cattle. "It's been a long time. Something about a woman couldn't be with the man she loves because she was... from the wrong side of the tracks. Low born." She shook her head. "Something like that anyway." She swallowed and glanced down at her saddle horn.

Jax chewed on his bottom lip, drummed his fingers on his thigh. He'd decided her answer would have to do when riders appeared on the horizon, snapping his mind right back to where it needed to be. Six men coming from Taylor's spread.

Molly and the other girls were a good six hundred yards away. Jax's signal to start moving the cattle was a waving hat. Now, the last thing he wanted was for them to get down in that ravine if these riders were bringing trouble. He squinted for a little better focus.

Cecelia followed his stare. "Friend or foe?"

"I'm not sure—" Motion pulled his attention back to the girls. Molly was charging down the hill toward the herd. "What the heck is she—?" The thunder of gunfire reached his ears. The Bar T riders kept coming, picking up their pace. Now Jax could see two of the men had their rifles out and were firing into the air. The others were whooping and hollering, and one of them cut loose with a ghostly, shrill Rebel Yell. Maria and Helen's horses panicked and launched down the hill, following Molly, away from the noise but toward the herd. "No, no, no—" Jax kicked Nickels, and in an instant, horse and rider were flying down the hill, over the sea of green.

In the narrow space at the confluence of the hills, the herd had turned, and fear was spreading through them like stink. Over his head, the gunfire kept up, was coming closer, though he couldn't see the men from down here. "This way, Maria! Helen!"

They couldn't hear him over the thundering guns. The herd broke and ran, and headed straight toward the girls, filling the air with the ominous thunder of thousands of hooves and a heavy dust cloud. Jax's heart hammered wildly at the imminent danger in front of Maria and Helen. He had to intercept them, get their attention, before they were too far in the draw to outrun the cattle. He whipped his reins back and forth over Nickels, desperate to get more speed from the animal. Maria and Helen had to see him and follow him up the hill, not up the middle of the draw where the herd would go.

Gunfire roared and boomed from the top of the ridge. What were these brushpoppers trying to do? Kill someone? Furious, Jax hunkered down and prayed for Nickels to run with everything he had in him. The horse was spread out to his full length, his hooves striking the ground fast as lightning. "Girls!" Jax yelled. "This way! This way!"

He leaped the small creek running between the hills. The herd bawled and bellowed, running blindly up the draw, leaving behind a cloud bank of dust. He saw Molly pull her horse up, spin him around in confusion. The first part of the herd rushed past her, obscuring her in its cloud. Jax prayed she could see him. "This way! Cross the ravine," he hollered, galloping toward Maria and Helen. He intercepted their path, fired his Colt to get their attention, sure they could hear it now and not the guns blazing on the ridge above. They did hear and gladly turned their horses to follow him, the pounding of the herd growing in volume, shaking the ground.

Where was Molly? Where was Cecelia? He glanced up. She had wisely stayed put at the top of the hill, but Twister was pawing, prancing, giving in to the panic in the air. She had his reins pulled back, hard to the left, keeping the horse in a tight circle. A moment later, Jax, Maria, and Helen lurched to a grass-shredding stop beside her. They watched the herd thunder up the creek between the two hills, not thirty feet below them. A minute later, the cattle disappeared over the top, headed for the canyons on the other side of the ridge.

Jax surveyed his *cowboys*. He'd never really looked down on the inexperienced hands. They all had to learn, but these girls— "You gave in to panic. You were running right for the herd."

Cecelia cut her eyes at him at his sharp tone.

"We were running from the gunshots," Helen fired back. Her eyes were wide with fear, her bony cheeks streaked with dirt. Beside her, the ever-quiet Maria merely sat still, breathing as hard as if she'd come up the hill on her own feet instead of in the saddle.

Jax settled back, bit down his irritation. The men from Taylor's spread were on the other side of the ravine, where the girls had been. Laughing and catcalling, they holstered their revolvers, slipped rifles back into scabbards. *Someone could have been hurt, and those yahoos...*

He didn't finish the thought. Instead, he whipped Nickels with the reins and the horse lunged down the hill, bounded across the creek, and skidded to a stop in the midst of the group, coming knee-to-knee with Woodward.

"Why, you look plumb mad, Jax." Woodward, no doubt at the center of the trouble, brought his hand to rest on his whip.

"Woodward, I hold you responsible for this. You could have got these girls killed with a stunt like that." Jax was so furious that he could barely control himself. All he wanted was to pound Woodward into the ground.

"Ah, Jax, you're wrong," one of the other cowboys mocked. "We wouldn't hurt those gals. We can see their curves from here."

Jax eyed the group. All new men. He didn't know any of them except Woodward, who'd been a hand at the Bar T when Jax left. All of them together spelled trouble.

Woodward's dirty-brown eyes narrowed as he tilted his hat back. A cold smile blossomed on his ugly, pockmarked face. "Just havin' a little fun at your hands' expense. Can't they handle a few hundred head stampeding?"

The men around them chuckled. Jax ground his teeth to keep from spouting profanity. No, this wasn't the first run-in with Woodward, but it was by far the worst, and he determined it would be the last. "You should have stayed in Florida. I warned you. In town, I warned you to keep to your own business."

Woodward straightened a touch. "You calling me out?"

"Get down off that horse."

Uncertainty twitched in Woodward's expression, pinched his brow, but his hand clenched the whip. "I ain't sure I should do that, I mean, you being who you are and—"

"Let me make it easy for you."

In one seemingly connected move, as Woodward snatched the whip off his hip, Jax grabbed hold of it. Holding onto the coiled leather with a death grip, he leaped from his saddle, launching into Woodward, slamming them both to the ground. Spooked horses squealed and pranced away from the two men who were entwined around each other like snakes, exchanging blows. Jax hated to fight but knew this was the only way to stop the harassment—or at least draw their attention solely to him.

He struggled to his feet, throwing a hard, hammer-of-a-blow to Woodward's jaw. The man's head snapped back, he staggered, and the whip fell from his fingers. Almost instantly, though, he shook off the daze and raised his fists again. Before they were clenched good, Jax stepped in with a jab, jab, and a devastating right hook. Blood gushed from the cowboy's nose and eyelid. He staggered drunkenly.

He was almost done, Jax guessed. But not quite.

Glaring at Jax, Woodward swung. Jax dodged it but felt the breeze, then hit the man with a vicious left hook, jarring his head and knocking loose a spattering of spit and blood. Woodward almost collapsed, but Jax grabbed his collar and reared back for another punch—

"Jax," Cecelia screamed from below them. "It's Molly!"

Jax wavered, saw the girls down the hill gathered around a body, and instantly slung Woodward off him. "You and your boys even look at somebody from the Burning Dress and I'll finish this." He purposely met the gaze of all the somber faces around him as he reclaimed the saddle. "Make sure Taylor knows what happened here and what I said."

He didn't wait for any responses as he and Nickels bolted down the hill.

CECELIA'S MOUTH fell open as she watched Jax race over and thrust himself into the middle of the hostile men. He went straight to one of them, the challenge clear in his posture and the snatches of angry voices she heard on the wind. Initially, she'd thought what a foolhardy thing to do, being outnumbered as he was. Was it a personal grudge? Or something noble? Was Jax trying to make himself the target of their shenanigans so the girls would go unmolested?

She and the others gasped when those angry voices changed to actions and Jax launched from the saddle, crashing into the other man, taking him to the ground with a thud that was clearly audible. Beside her, Maria gasped again and pointed down the hill. "It's Molly."

As if they were all one being, the three girls kicked their horses simultaneously and raced toward the body lying at the bottom of the draw. As they thundered through the thick grass, Cecelia looked over and saw Jax grab the man by his collar. She admired his courage, his obvious goal of keeping those men focused on him, but Molly needed him in one piece and right now. Could he get out of the fight?

"Jax," she cried, Twister in a wide-open gallop, "It's Molly!"

He reacted so quickly to her call, ending the fight and leaping into the saddle, that he nearly beat the girls to their fallen comrade. The mocking laughter of the men on the ridge echoed down to her as they all dismounted and rushed to Molly's aid. An instant later, Jax was there, dismounting Nickels before the horse had come to a stop. Again, Cecelia was impressed by his concern for his hands. It struck her as...noble.

Molly was lying face down, a few feet from the creek, one bloody hand twisted at an odd angle and lying in the small of her back. "You girls keep an eye on the ridge." Jax knelt beside her, carefully repositioned the arm, and rolled her over. Molly groaned softly and the group breathed a little easier over the sign of life. Her face was smeared with blood. Mud and blood marred her shirt and chaps.

"Molly!" Jax leaned into her face. "Molly, can you hear me?"

The girl's eyes fluttered open. A moment passed before she focused on him. "Yeah…I hear you," she whispered hoarsely.

Jax moved her hair, checked her skull. "Where do you hurt?"

"Besides all over?"

Cecelia smiled. Humor had to be a good sign. Jax nodded and said tenderly, "Yeah. Besides all over."

"My head. My nose." She managed to drop a hand on her face, lightly pressing her fingers to her forehead. "The riders startled Leo. He panicked, then threw me."

"So, you weren't in the stampede?" Cecelia asked.

Molly shook her head. "Pretty much ran by me. Don't know where Leo got off to, though."

Jax peeled out of his gloves. "Well, let's make sure your nose is the worst of it." He drifted his hands over the patient, checking for broken ribs or limbs. "Maria, you and Helen get back to the ranch and bring the wagon. And double-time it." The women moved as if the command had come from God Himself, mounting their horses and disappearing over the other ridge in a matter of seconds.

Satisfied that Molly's injuries weren't any worse, he looked over at Cecelia. "Why don't you hold her head off the ground, and I'll see what I've got to cover her."

Cecelia was also quick to do as he asked, and a moment later, he returned with a wool poncho. He spread it over Molly and even tucked it around her as if she were a sleeping toddler. Cecelia wondered at his compassion as she shifted to better cradle Molly's head. And then chastised herself for reading too much into his behavior. William, always somewhat aloof, hadn't been cruel until the moment he'd learned of her *disability*. But then he had changed as abruptly as a candle extinguished by the wind.

"I ain't cold," Molly said, frowning.

Jax tucked the poncho beneath her chin, nonetheless. "Can't let you get cold, either. Now, you just keep talking till that wagon gets here." He slipped his gaze to Cecelia. "I'll be right back. Don't let her fall asleep."

"Molly, you're sure nothing else hurts?" Cecelia asked, and then carried on a disjointed conversation with the patient, while at the same time watching Jax ride to the top of the other hill, survey the area, and then come back down.

"They're gone."

"Molly, you missed it. You should have seen Jax here teach those boys a lesson."

"A lesson?"

"Before he realized you were hurt, he rode right up into the middle of them." Cecelia was talking to Molly, but watching Jax's face. "Like a knight, ready for battle." A pink hue tinged his cheeks, and Cecelia had to fight a grin. "He schooled one of them quite well with a few appropriately placed strikes."

"Oh, my," Molly said breathlessly. "Wish I'd seen."

"Yeah, well, it wasn't much of a show." Jax pulled

his hat off and mopped his face and neck with his bandana. "But I don't reckon they'll be picking on you girls anymore."

Cecelia thought that was a vain hope and exchanged a dark glance with Jax. An unexpected righteous anger and a sense of protectiveness welled up within her. He couldn't be a sacrificial lamb when it most likely wouldn't help in the end. "If we stick together, they won't trouble any of us."

Jax paused as he was dropping his hat in place, then he inclined his head a touch, and a slight smile lifted the corner of his mouth. "You're probably right."

CECELIA DID NOT HEAD in with the wagon carrying Molly. Instead, she thought she could be of more use staying behind to look for Leo, the girl's horse. Not that she didn't care about Molly. Not that she cared about the horse more. She simply didn't care for the drama. Virginia crying on her shoulder had filled Cecelia's quota of emotion for the next year. Besides, there was nothing she could do to help. Why be in the way? Rather than discuss it, she faded off as the wagon headed back to the Burning Dress.

She rode for an hour across the swaying, undulating hills of grass with no sound but an eerie wind whistling in her ears. Eventually, her mind wandered, drifted to dark thoughts. *What-ifs* buffeted her like constant gusts of prairie wind. What if the men from the Bar T had rolled right over Jax? What if Jax hadn't been there at all? What if Molly had been killed?

What if the Bar T men came back?

Now...here?

Cecelia let her gaze sweep over the vast, open, and hauntingly desolate landscape and realized how alone she was. Bar T men could be right behind the next hill. What would they do if they found her by herself? Heart racing, Cecelia pressed on, stumbling across Leo, and then eventually Lowdy's crew, which worked a great sigh of relief from her.

She assumed they had been dispatched to make sure the herd went into the box canyon and not over on the Bar T land. Lowdy and four hands, all women, were gathered at the canyon entrance, the cattle having gone exactly where intended. The cowboy's white hair flashed as he removed his hat to wipe his forehead. Cecelia and the horses jogged over.

He nodded politely as she rode up. "Sounded like Molly was probably gonna be all right."

"I think so. She was talking and said she'd been thrown, not caught in the stampede." Not that one couldn't be just as deadly as the other. "I thought I might be more helpful looking for her horse."

Lowdy's features tightened up. "I ain't heard all the details, but I reckon you shouldn't go riding around alone. Jax might have calmed Taylor's boys down some or stirred up a hornet's nest. 'Til we know, you should be careful."

Cecelia considered the warning and the fact that her pulse was just now slowing. "He rode right into them, hard and fast. I thought he did it to draw attention from us."

"Sounds like Jax."

"You could argue it was a little hot-headed." *If you wanted to find something to nit-pick.*

"Maybe you could. I wouldn't."

Cecelia lowered her gaze, sorry to have offended the man.

Lowdy pulled a can of snuff from his back pocket. "Jax don't usually look for a fight, but"—he offered Cecelia the can, but she waved it away politely, appreciative of the peace offering—"I'm gonna guess he had his reasons and stand with him."

"Fair enough."

"We'll be heading back pretty soon." He pressed a pinch of tobacco into his lip. "I think you should stay and ride in with us."

"All right." She wasn't inclined to head off alone again. She didn't think a person needed to be a genius to know a group of cowboys riding up on a lone female from the Burning Dress was more than enough fuel to start a fire.

CHAPTER SEVEN

By the time Cecelia finished putting Twister and Leo up for the night, she had missed dinner. At least, the central meal in the dining hall. Maude fed her and the other girls who had come in late in the kitchen. They gathered around a large wooden island, chatted politely, but Cecelia was bone-tired. One girl, Milleta, a bronzed, husky half-Indian, half-Spanish farmer from Nacogdoches, seemed intent on keeping the conversation going when it hit a lull. When she wasn't peppering the exhausted crew with questions, she was busy offering bland details of her life on the Rio Grande and thoughts on Burning Dress.

Cecelia tried to listen, to keep her mind on something other than her ride across the prairie today, but it haunted her. She hadn't tasted fear like that in a long time.

Before today, she'd still felt mostly disconnected from the ranch. Virginia had smiled her silly smile and shared her heartbreaking story, wheedling at least a little way into Cecelia's heart. She was sure she'd think of her every so often in the years to come. And she hoped Virginia would find peace.

Besides the connection with Virginia, however, Cecelia had felt as if she were a ghost here, floating past the women like Milleta, no connection to them, just hovering around them till something happened.

The cold, biting fear in her heart today had changed that. Her vulnerability out there on the prairie had pinched her, like someone waking her from a dream. This was real, and she needed to keep her wits about her. She didn't need to make friends, but she needed to accept that she shouldn't do this alone.

AFTER BATHING and popping in to check on Molly—an action Cecelia acknowledged was more obligatory than born of compassion—she took a torn shirt and her sewing kit and went in search of a quiet corner.

For a big house with so many people in it, she was surprised to find a small library empty, but an inviting fire burning in its stone fireplace. Miss Sally had said no room was off limits, other than her office and bedroom. Grateful for the solitude, Cecelia settled into a large, leather chair and began repairing the sleeve partially torn loose from the bodice.

Sewing always relaxed her, gave her mind time to wander. If she didn't have to live in such communal conditions, she thought she might truly enjoy ranching. She just didn't want to get to know the people here beyond a work relationship. She wanted to be left alone and not establish friendships. Friends here would be the same as friends in Atlanta.

Her fingers slowed then stopped. The anger at William that she tried to keep wound up like a ball of yarn loosened a little, revealing her underlying hurt.

She blinked, went back to her sewing. Of course, she was hurt. Anyone would be after—

"Mind if I sit for a few minutes?"

She looked up at the door. Jax, freshly washed and shaved, dressed in clean, black duds, his dark hair still curling from the damp, leaned on the frame. He fanned his cowboy hat in his hand, but in a jerky manner, as if he was trying to look calm and relaxed but wasn't in reality. Cecelia seriously considered asking him to let her be, but then he stepped into the room.

"I can see by the look on your face you'd rather be alone, but I'd like a woman's opinion on something."

She acquiesced with a grudging nod and stopped her sewing. Jax dropped in the matching chair a few feet from her, but leaned forward, perching on the edge of the seat. Come to think of it, she wanted to ask him something as well. "Tell me something, first. That fight today. What do you think will come of it?" Her ride alone on the prairie stalked her with its fear and *what-ifs*. "Lowdy wonders if you've stirred up a hornet's nest. He didn't want me riding around alone."

Jax sucked in a deep breath, rotated his hat around

and around for a moment, buying time to answer, she suspected.

"I've got a grudge with the Bar T. What I did today was make sure they understood the fight's with me. Not any of you. Don't know if they'll listen."

"How long have you been with Miss Sally?"

"Little over a year."

A suspicion formed in Cecelia's mind. "Where were you before you came here?"

The pregnant pause was her answer, but he replied, "The Bar T."

"Falling out with the boss or his men?"

"You could say I don't get along too well with Taylor."

"Oh." And Cecelia had stumbled into learning more about Jax than she wanted to know. Another tentacle to draw her in. "Then we should be cautious?"

"Don't stray too far from the ranch. If you need to go anywhere iffy, ride with somebody. I don't think Taylor ordered what happened today, but I do know there are no saints working for him, and a woman alone could be tempting prey."

Prey. Trash to be used and tossed away. Not much difference in the end. William's throaty voice boomed in her head. *"What good are you to anyone? You are worthless, a failure. Well, I'll not be burdened by you."*

"What did he do to you?"

She snapped back to Jax, uncomfortable with the expression of pity on his face. "What?"

"Sorry." He twisted his hat cruelly. "None of my business. I just know that look."

"Look?"

"Anger masks the pain. But the mask slips every now and again."

Cecelia refused to talk about this. She wouldn't think about William. She certainly wouldn't discuss him with another man. "Are we safe? You said we shouldn't ride alone."

"Some place you wanna go?"

"No. Merely in the course of business or just riding to town, I wanted to know how paranoid we should be."

"I don't like the word paranoid. It'll make you jittery. Folks'll be jumping at shadows."

"I'm sure after what happened today, no one will be paranoid." Her tone was curt, even condescending, but she didn't apologize.

"Right."

Then, wasn't she being a bit of a hypocrite? Nerves *had* almost gotten the better of her today. She'd been jumping at shadows before she'd found Lowdy's crew.

He rubbed his neck and sighed. "I'll talk to Taylor. Make sure he keeps those dogs on a short rope."

Cecelia supposed that was all he could do.

"My turn," he said. "Tell me about the song."

"The song?" *The French song?* "You're like a bulldog. We talked about it."

"I talked. You danced. Around the truth."

His stare made her uncomfortable—intent, forthright, but masking pain. Ah. He knew the look because he wore it sometimes, too. "You used the pronoun *she*. '*She* used to hum it.' Obviously, she hurt you somehow. I didn't want to rub salt in the wound."

With a disgusted-sounding grunt, he looked down at his hands, started to scrunch his hat, but stopped himself. "Why don't you let me worry about that?"

Well, he wasn't going to let go of this. And Cecelia was tired. "Fine. It's the story of a woman who pretends to love a man to get at another man. She's a —a confidence artist. A thief. And then she falls in love with the first man and can't be with him because of her past."

A moment passed without his reply, the only sound the popping, hissing fire. Finally, he said, "All that in one short song?"

"Near as I recall. I can't remember the lyrics. Hence, the reason for *humming*." She didn't mean to be so sharp with Jax, but it had been a long day, and she didn't appreciate his glimpse into her life and vice versa. He made her...uncomfortable somehow.

"Love sure is a miserable thing, ain't it?" he muttered.

"I wouldn't give you a nickel for it." Her bitter tone brought his head up. She fought the urge to apologize or look away from a gaze that was filled with curiosity, hurt, and surprise.

He grunted. "Yeah, me neither." Then his brow furrowed and his gaze frosted over. "I think Miss Sally broke a man's heart."

Cecelia wanted to drop her head in her hands and scream. She didn't care. She didn't want these details about anyone. She wanted to repair her shirt and go to bed. Not get drawn in by stories or captivating blue eyes—

"In her case," he continued, "I think she did it as kindly as possible—"

"Jax, please," she interrupted. Her plea was for him to stop, but also for her to have the strength to push him away. Cecelia sensed a vulnerability when she was around Jax, and it worried her. She needed distance from him.

He stopped, seemed to realize he was rambling, and surged to his feet. "I'm sorry. Yeah. Well, goodnight."

"No, I'm sorry. I don't mean to be short. I'm just tired." Which was still no excuse for rude behavior… "Virginia told me about the buttons you bought. I'd be happy to sew them on for you," she said as a peace offering.

He spun his hat around for a second, but then shook his head. "'Preciate it, but I've got it covered."

"All right then. Goodnight."

When he was gone, Cecelia stared into the fire, wondering about the woman who had sung this song to Jax. Almost as if she had been trying to tell him the truth about her?

And what to make of the nugget about Miss Sally's love life? Did it explain why she wasn't married at her age? Had she been hurt, like the women she brought to the ranch?

Love.

What an awful, terrible emotion.

Cecelia's mask slipped again. Her chin quivered and tears threatened. No woman wanted to be treated as if she were worthless, of no value, with nothing to contribute to a home. *"Tell me, my dear, what does it feel like to be a failure?"* he'd asked her so coolly one day on the veranda. And the verbal barrage had gone on for months. Until the moment the doctor delivered the final diagnosis. Benign tumor. No children. Ever.

She swallowed. William and his arrogant, lifted chin, tailored clothes, high expectations of everyone around him. How dare she disappoint? But with the grounds certain and legal, his waiting had ended. The divorce had been swift and final. Complete before she even left the church's basement.

Angrily wiping tears from her eyes, she glanced around the small library, most of it hidden in flickering shadows. She couldn't believe she was here. On a ranch. Moving cattle. This was absurd. She was a teacher. She should go back to teaching French and German. Settle into a nice preparatory school and torture students until she was an eighty-year-old spinster.

She leaned her head on the back of the chair. Yes, eventually, she would return to the classroom. For now, moving those cattle, thundering across the open prairie at a wide-open gallop, working with her hands, staying outdoors all day, and, yes, tolerating others who were surviving their own hurts—it wasn't awful. She wasn't the only one here who love had scorned. She wasn't alone.

If she were a failure, at least she had company.

CHAPTER EIGHT

CECELIA WATCHED FROM THE DORM ROOM WINDOW AS the wagon pulled out, loaded with a dozen frilly, bonneted women on their way to church. Miss Sally was in the driver's seat. Of course, they had all invited Cecelia—again—but she had politely declined. She dropped the curtain and turned toward the mostly empty dorm. Mostly. A few girls slept in, their heads buried in the blankets.

Cecelia sighed, bored. Restless. Lowdy's warning and her personal fears still echoed in her ears, but her nerves had settled. A ride across the dewy grass called to her, and she answered. She would stay close to the house though.

Enticed by the lovely way to spend a Sunday morning, she dressed and headed for the barn. She was nearly at the entrance when she heard voices from the side and stopped short. Two men were talking with what she would describe as agitation.

The tone wasn't raised, but the heightened emotion was obvious. However, she wasn't close enough to make out words.

Carefully, she walked over to the edge of the barn and peered around the corner. Between the barn and the corral, Jax and a tall, older gentleman, both in profile, were whispering and gesticulating with curt, angry movements. The more they argued, the more their anger seemed to grow. Just as Cecelia decided to back away, the older man spun to his horse, snatched the reins free from the corral fence, and heaved into the saddle.

He spared one burning glance at Jax and kicked his mount to a gallop, headed out the back way across the northern meadow. Cecelia was immediately envious of the man's ease in the saddle. He was like a song, so harmonious and rhythmic, in tune with the sorrel. A born horseman. Who was he? And why had he and Jax been arguing?

She cleared her throat and stepped out from behind the barn. "Looks like a good idea. I think I'll take a ride, too."

Sneering, Jax snatched off his hat and smacked it against his thigh. He followed the man with a fierce glare. "You know who that is?"

"No idea."

"Taylor. He figured he'd come see me before I rode over to his spread."

"You really were going to go over there? That seems the height of foolishness."

Something changed in Jax's expression. Confusion replaced the anger and he rotated a shoulder. "I…uh, they wouldn't have done anything. Especially if I was there to see Taylor."

"So, is he going to do anything to rein in his men?"

"He gave it lip service."

"His hands stampeded our cattle, got Molly hurt. They could have gotten her killed. He has to do something to those men."

"Said he'll see who might have been involved and give 'em their pay. At the very least, he promised no more trouble."

"Is he a man of his word?" Was there such a thing?

"Nope," Jax said flatly. "He'll look you in the eye and lie right to your face."

"Oh." But somehow, Cecelia had the feeling Jax's observation was aimed at something more than the current situation.

He snugged his hat back in place and turned to her. "You fixin' to go for a ride? I don't recommend it. Not alone."

"I wasn't going to go far." Then Cecelia noticed Jax's clean clothes, still all black, string tie, his shaved face, the Bible resting on top of the fence post, and Nickels saddled and ready a few feet away. "Were you going somewhere?"

"I was headed to church. You should come."

Cecelia backed up a step. "Maybe some other time."

"Well, then, will you wait? We can go for a nice

ride when I get back." Two of them? Perhaps a touch of concern or confusion over the meaning of the offer showed on her face. He plucked his Bible from the post. "I'd be willing to bet Miss Sally and several of the other girls would like to go. Maybe we'll even have a picnic."

She breathed a sigh of relief…laced with a little disappointment. "For a picnic, I can wait."

AND SHE WAS glad of the decision. Those who didn't want to ride horseback took the wagon, and twenty Burning Dress Ranch hands spread out on the sun-washed meadow overlooking the babbling Spanish Fork. Some dined on ham biscuits, some lay back and snoozed in the warmth. Three of the girls had donned parasols and sat staring out at the Big Horn Mountains and their craggy, white tips scraping the cloudless sky. Lowdy and Bug were tossing a baseball back and forth, their awkward attempt at trying the new sport.

Cecelia chuckled as Lowdy missed the toss to him and jogged off into the tall grass to retrieve the ball. Reclining on the blanket with her, Miss Sally, Virginia, and Wilhelma enjoyed their biscuits, a little of the licorice from town, and an apple pie.

The big German girl dragged her fork around her tin plate, intent on getting the last of the crumbs. "Apple pie and licorice is not so good together. *Yuk.*"

Cecelia and Virginia winked at each other. "Didn't

bother me none," Virginia said. "I was tickled to have the sweet treats."

Miss Sally finished the last bite of her biscuit and wiped the crumbs off her mouth and hands. "For a last-minute picnic, I think we've done all right."

"Well, I'm gonna follow it up with a wade in the river." Virginia gained her feet and smoothed her dress. For a moment, Cecelia feared Virginia might see her daughter in the water, but the girl smiled and worked off her lace-up boots.

Is she facing her fears? Cecelia wondered.

"*Yah*, I think I'll go, too." Wilhelma removed her shoes, rose, and the two women meandered down to the water. Cecelia watched them for a minute, but her attention drifted over to Jax. The horses were tied to a picket line strung from the wagon to a cedar. He was slicing an apple and feeding pieces of it to Nickels. Miss Sally opened her mouth as if to speak, but was interrupted by Maude and another older woman from the garden crew.

Maude knelt beside Miss Sally. "We wanted to talk about Cara Newman's baby."

Miss Sally grimaced. "Such a tragedy. Breaks my heart."

"Well, we wanted to pass the hat at supper tonight and help pay for the funeral. If you don't mind."

"Of course not. I'll be the first to throw in."

Apparently satisfied with the answer, Maude fought age and stiff knees and finally, with the other woman's help, worked back to her feet. "I'm gettin' too old for sitting on the ground."

"Now, now," Miss Sally chided, touching Maude's knee. "You're only as old as you think, and I think you have a spring in your step."

Maude's expression of pain changed to surprise and then happiness. "Strange." She rubbed her right knee. "All of a sudden, I do feel better. Thank you for the kind words, Miss Sally."

The two wandered off to where the sad baseball practice was happening. Cecelia had heard some of the girls talking about the Newmans' baby. An infant who had died suddenly at only three days old.

"Life is a hard row to hoe, isn't it?" Miss Sally observed sadly.

Cecelia plucked a piece of grass and fiddled with it. "Isn't for the faint of heart, that's for sure." For some reason, this thought dragged her gaze back to Jax, still pampering his horse. "I can't believe he was thinking about going to see Taylor. Anything could have happened. Especially if there are hard feelings between him and this Mr. Taylor."

Miss Sally's forehead creased in a pained expression. "He would have been all right. I'm surprised Quitman made the trip over to see *him*."

"They both looked pretty angry, but it ended peaceably enough. Though Jax didn't sound happy with the parting. He wasn't convinced Taylor would keep his men under control." She frowned with the memory. "There's more going on than this tiff, isn't there?" Not that it was her place to discuss it.

Miss Sally heaved a long, heavy sigh. "That boy has a lot of forgiving to do."

"I gather it has something to do with a French girl."

Miss Sally dropped her gaze and pawed at some lint on the blanket. "Jax will have to tell you his story himself."

"Oh, I wasn't asking or trying to, you know..." *Get involved.* "Gossip."

"I will say he's making progress." For some reason, Miss Sally bounced her gaze back and forth between Jax and Cecelia, and her sad expression turned to something Cecelia couldn't read. Curiosity, perhaps? "The ones closest to you—when they hurt you—forgiving is even harder."

"I suppose."

"If you can come to understand what Jesus did on the cross—the incredible sacrifice—it makes humbling yourself a little easier. You have to be humble to forgive. But it's so freeing to live without the bitterness."

Cecelia thought of Tallulah and the night she'd burned her dress. The woman genuinely seemed to have dropped a weight and was eager to soar into her future. Cecelia, however, didn't see how talk of forgiveness applied to her. She didn't hate William. She wasn't bitter at all. She'd gotten past the betrayal. She was perfectly fine.

She ripped the little blade of grass into several pieces. "I think the things you're telling Virginia are helping her." *At least.*

"Sweet Virginia. Such a tragedy about her daughter. But she...you, me, Jax...we're all so precious to the

Lord. He loves us dearly, and I'm so grateful that love is unconditional. It doesn't rely on good works. It's not broken by terrible mistakes." She narrowed her eyes at Cecelia. "It's not voided by harsh, ugly words. We are priceless works of art to God. Fearfully and wonderfully made. Virginia is coming to understand the impact of His love. You will, too, in time."

Cecelia almost scoffed. Love. Deep or shallow, she preferred never to discuss it. In part, from her betrayal, but also because she simply couldn't imagine a love like that. *What would things be like? How would it change your life,* she wondered, *if such pure love existed?*

Better not indulge in fantasy. Cecelia just wanted to be left alone. Do her job. Learn a skill. And move on.

But, to what? This one question—what did her future hold now?—hung her up repeatedly.

"The answers will come in time," Miss Sally said.

"I'm sorry?" Cecelia felt as if she'd missed some part of the conversation.

Miss Sally smiled. "Nothing."

Cecelia decided to turn the conversation. "How did you come to own the Burning Dress?"

"It was a gift from my father."

"He must be fairly wealthy."

"Exceedingly."

"And he must have quite a bit of confidence in you to run it. How long have you been here?"

"How long?" She took a deep breath, shrugged a shoulder. "Feels like forever."

Cecelia perceived Miss Sally was being coy with

her answers and wondered why. Did the woman know about the things folks in town said about her and the ranch? Did that make her careful with her words, with the information she shared? She risked another question. "I still don't know how the ranch got its name. Will you tell me?"

Miss Sally took a long time to answer, but somehow Cecelia knew she would. "Years ago, I had a friend. She was betrothed to a man of whom her father did not approve. At all. They were forbidden to marry. They were forbidden to even speak to each other. Despite her father's orders, she continued to build a relationship with the young man. Then he asked her to marry him.

"Unfortunately, at around the same time, the young man fell in with some bad companions and was caught up in something terrible. The girl's father knew all along..." Her blank stare said she had drifted into a different time. "He knew all along the boy would make the wrong choice."

She blinked, coming back to Cecelia. "My friend was heartbroken. Not just over the young man, but that she'd disobeyed her father, when, if she'd listened to him, he could have saved her so much heartache and grief. She swore to never disobey him again and burned her wedding dress.

"So, I ask the girls to burn their gowns when they're ready to let go of their hurts, to let go of being an earthly bride and instead choose to become the bride of Christ. To promise to put Him first."

Cecelia mulled over the story. And found she still had questions. "Do they swear off men?"

"Only if they want to. If the Lord leads them. But others will find that putting Christ at the head of a marriage—of any relationship—makes the bond sweet and unbreakable."

CHAPTER NINE

THE CHAT WITH MISS SALLY LEFT CECELIA RESTLESS, and she wandered down to the stream to be alone. Keeping everyone at arm's length had seemed so easy at first. The plan to avoid entanglements meant no chance at heartache and betrayal. Don't establish any friendships. Be polite but keep your distance. Virginia, with her big, surprised eyes and shattered heart, had altered the plan. She tugged at Cecelia's heartstrings. A little further off in the distance was Jax. Something about him tugged at her, too, but the pull wasn't overwhelming. Yet. She could still leave Burning Dress without looking back.

She picked up a stone as she meandered beside the water.

The belief made her future look so...bleak. But safe.

Yet...she had to wonder. Would she ever live with the kind of joy she'd seen in Tallulah's eyes the night of the fire? Audacious, fearless, willing...*vulnerability*.

The thought made her shiver and she tossed the stone into the water. The ramifications were terrifying. Vulnerability, sharing your heart, letting people close opened the door to all the lies that masqueraded as love, friendship, and loyalty. She couldn't go through that again. Nothing was worth the risk.

Frustrated, she shook away all these deep, philosophical ruminations and stepped over a downed log. Up ahead, a huge, flat, sun-washed boulder protruded out into the laughing water. Cecelia was glad she'd worn dungarees and quickly made her way to the rock. No skirt to hike up out of the water, no cloth tangling around her legs. She was going to lie down and nap—

She was only a few feet away from him when she realized Jax was sitting on a smaller rock, Bible open on his lap, his eyes closed, his mouth moving slightly. Cecelia flinched, embarrassed at stumbling blindly into the man's private time. He hadn't seen her at least.

She took a few quiet steps backward, hoping the water was covering the crunch of gravel beneath her boots, then turned. She'd not realized he was such a passionate, church-going man. He didn't beat anyone over the head with his faith.

Well, unless you were another man attempting to bring harm to Burning Dress Ranch women. Then Jax was happy to beat you over the head with anything handy. He was no soft-spoken milquetoast.

She chuckled and simultaneously heard what sounded like a snort up ahead. She stopped abruptly, her body locking up like rusty gears, except for her mouth, which fell open in a silent scream. Not thirty feet away, a husky, shimmering black bear ambled from the stream, grumbled at her, and climbed up on the bank. Directly in her path.

Every fiber of Cecelia's being felt as if it had become thin, fragile glass and was about to shatter in a million pieces. Her heart hammered wildly in her chest, but the blood in her veins felt thick and heavy. Her mouth was frozen in a scream that she wished more than anything she could free.

Oh, God, was all she could manage as the bear turned to her, his mammoth paws splayed on the ground, nose sniffing the air. He could smell her fear. How could he not? His eyes glimmered with challenge. Then, like a behemoth, he stood up on his hind legs and roared, a deafening, angry reverberation of his supremacy.

She was going to faint. Cecelia was going to faint dead away, and this bear was going to eat her—

"Aaaaaaagh!" Jax launched past Cecelia, roaring, waving his Bible in one hand, his gun in the other, belching fire and thunder into the air. The heavy, booming sound of the big .44 echoed like a fierce summer storm all around them. The bear dropped to all fours, taken aback by the crazy man wielding the power of sound and fury, charging wild-eyed toward him like a grizzly. The animal shook his head, whined, and leaped into the water, bounding and splashing away from the noisome humans. Jax yelled one more time from the edge of the water. Fired a final shot.

With the echo of the Colt, the bear disappeared into the trees on the other side.

Cecelia was frozen, mindless with fear, panic, and relief. Yes, relief. The ice paralyzing her muscles began to melt as she replayed the image of Jax running past her, arms waving over his head. The gun in one hand, a Bible in the other. Slowly, the shock gave way to laughter. It bubbled up, a little hysterical at first, but when Jax turned to look at her, sapphire eyes wide with concern, real humor seeped in. She was laughing, almost cackling. "Oh, I wish." She shook her head, the humor stealing her breath. "I wish you could have seen…" She was laughing and crying.

He *had* looked like a crazy man. She doubled over, holding her aching sides. "You looked like a madman. No wonder the bear…" She straightened up and, for a split second, was able to hold a stern look. "It was the Bible," she said melodramatically, pointing her index finger at him and collapsing into gales of hysterical laughter. She could see the pages flapping in the black leather book, and then Jax was laughing, too. "What were you going to…to do? Throw the Good Book at him if you ran out of bullets?" That struck her as even funnier. In the next moment, they were both sitting on the ground, leaning on one another, still laughing, tears on their cheeks…until their eyes met. The laughter faded awkwardly. Her breathing calmed.

Cecelia realized with a jolt what Jax had done and pulled away from him. "You saved my life."

"Nah, I just…" He scratched his nose, folded the Bible to his chest. "Just did what I had to do."

To save me, she thought. He would have done it for anybody, she understood, but he had done it for *her*. His compassion, his courage, his willingness to put himself in harm's way for another human impacted her. She couldn't say how exactly, though. William, she was quite sure, would have never risked his life for her. Not even at the beginning of their marriage. She cleared her throat and stood up, brushing off her jeans. He stood as well, resting his hand on the butt of the holstered gun.

"You saved my life," she whispered, nauseous over the realization that if not for Jax, she could be a mangled, bloody dinner in a bear's mouth right now.

She shivered and he draped an arm around her. "Here now, let's get back. They're probably wondering what all the shooting was about."

IN THE MOMENT he'd seen the bear preparing to charge Cecelia, Jax had prayed and would have sworn he'd summoned the strength to rip the animal apart with his bare hands, had it been necessary. Underlying the courageous charge had been a galvanizing fear. The vision of the bear sinking its teeth into Cecelia's defenseless body had put proverbial wings on his feet.

His arm around her now, the warmth of her close to him, he was dumbfounded and weak-kneed. She was so small and fragile. Such a tiny thing. He'd never been so determined to face danger, give everything, even his own life, to save someone—not even the wisp of a second thought, only the absolutely certainty he would die for her if necessary.

Oh, he would have fought to save any of his friends, but this felt very different.

He stole a glance at her and sighed quietly. The emotions roiling in his chest nearly sucked the breath out of him. He had feelings for Cecelia. But they were wrong and pointless. *Lord, thank you for letting me save her. But she's not a Believer. And I know better than to repeat that mistake.*

CECELIA MOVED like a ghost around Twister as she unwound his reins from the picket line. In her head, she kept seeing that bear charging at her, snarling, spittle flying from its mouth. Jax, coming out of nowhere, charging toward the animal, inserting himself between her and the danger. No one had ever done anything like that for her.

And then he'd put his arm around her, and she'd calmed instantly. His presence was comforting, his touch was...warm. Peaceful.

She mounted Twister and backed the horse away from the rope. Of course, she reminded herself again, Jax didn't make the brave sacrifice specifically *for her*. She wouldn't flatter herself. *Jax has something in his character—*

"You all right?" he asked, riding up beside her.

"Yeah, I'm—" She shivered. "I'll probably have a nightmare or two, but I'll be all right."

"Yeah, you will."

She looked at him sideways, unsure of his meaning. He winked, and she lowered her head, releasing some more tension. "Why did you do it? I just can't seem to understand."

"You're making a lot out of it. After all, *I* had the gun. Not the bear."

She chuckled weakly. "True." Why couldn't she understand this man? Why could she still feel his arm around her? "You rode into those fellows from Bar T the other day like—like bait. Intent on drawing them off us. You flew down the hill when I screamed that Molly was hurt. I don't…I just don't understand you." He was different, so very different from any man she'd ever known. But why? How? What was there about him that…gave her this peaceful feeling? Admittedly, even before the bear incident.

"I don't know if I can make things plain to you. I don't think you'll understand it yet."

Yet?

"Scripture says there is no greater love than a man would lay down his life for his friends."

"I'm not your friend."

"No."

Again, she'd been needlessly brusque. It cut him, she could tell, and she wilted a little. Why did she turn into barbed wire around this man?

He sucked on his teeth for a moment, then said,

"Well, how 'bout this: I try to consider others more important than myself."

He added nothing else, and she shook her head. "Why?"

"Cecelia..." He pulled his horse up, and she followed suit. "The only answer I can give you is..." He turned to her, studied her face, searched her eyes intently, as if looking for an answer as well...or perhaps wondering if she could receive his. "I've lived without Jesus. Now I live with Him. In my heart. In my soul. If you let Him, He can change everything about you. For the better. And bring peace and joy I can't describe."

Cecelia wasn't sure she wanted everything about her changed. But she kept her scoffing to herself. Before her was a man who believed everything good in him came from a relationship with a Savior. Who was she to mock where he found courage, peace...joy?

But his comments showed her an obvious conundrum. "Jax, if you are so full of this Savior, how is it that you don't want to love anyone?"

He blinked and gave her a bewildered look. "I just don't want..." His brow furrowed as he seemed to ponder the question.

Obviously, she had troubled him with the challenge to his logic.

"I guess I want to love from a distance," he muttered, his expression darkening, as if the answer was wrong or at least troubling.

"What's wrong with that?" she asked. "As long as you're a good person, don't lie, hurt others, or—like you said—you're willing to lay down your life for another, you don't have to get so tangled up with people."

"Yeah. I guess..."

Unable to understand why he seemed to doubt the idea, she swallowed, nodded slightly, and nudged Twister forward. Not getting tangled up with people. Such was her plan, and while it wasn't working perfectly, she would get out of Burning Dress without an ensnared heart, so help her.

CHAPTER TEN

A WARM JULY BREEZE DRIFTED OVER THE SWAYING alfalfa like a lover's hands, and Cecelia smiled. Up to Twister's chest, this rolling, rich emerald valley of grass had room for twice the cattle they were watching over today. *Another thousand would fit here easy,* she thought. *No wonder the Bar T boys are jealous.*

Speaking of boys…

She, Maria, Helen, and Molly each had vantage points high on the hills, watching the herd but watching out for the troublemakers from the other ranch, as well. The boy she watched now, however, was Jax. He'd ridden out, approached each of the girls separately, chatted a few minutes, and then headed back. Without speaking to Cecelia. He'd merely waved and kept riding.

And this was not the first time this week he'd distanced himself from her. He'd walked past her with nothing more than a nod or a hat tip and sent her out with Lowdy's crew twice now, instead of his. More than that, though, he'd kept his conversations with her clipped, instructions succinct. She wasn't imagining it. Jax was avoiding her.

Did the bear incident have something to do with it? Had she not been appropriately grateful? True, she was not one to gush and carry on, but maybe he had expected a bit more of an *effusive* thank you. Did he think her ungrateful?

Of course, what Jax thought about her level of emotive expression didn't matter a whit to Cecelia. Only, she *was* grateful. The word was such a weak euphemism for how she truly felt, she wished she could come up with a new one. She wasn't bear scat at this moment thanks to Jax, and she was so appreciative she could kiss him, wait on him hand and foot, walk behind him with a fan. Anything he wanted. Yet, after Sunday, she hadn't mentioned his rescue again—hadn't really had the chance—but she could have found a way to say a nice thank you one more time.

Cecelia exhaled, straightened in the saddle, and turned her mind back to work, determined to speak with Jax this evening. Only, the feel of his arm around her, the heat of his body next to hers, weakened her resolve. Maybe she should just stay away from him…

Oh, you're being foolish. Say thank you one more time, clear the air, and be done with this waffling.

THE EVENING SONG of crickets and frogs nearly drowned out the lowing of cattle as Cecelia made her way to the bunkhouse. The heat of the day was gone, having fallen to cooler, mountain temperatures. She wrapped her shawl a little tighter around her, wishing she were in her robe and headed to bed instead of the men's quarters. This trip had necessitated a dress, of course, rather than night clothes, though she sorely wanted to be settling down for the evening.

First things first, however.

As she approached the porch, in its shadows, she saw an orange glow arc up, pause, come back down. A moment later, smoke swirled out of the dark. One of the hands was enjoying a smoke. Most of them were here during the week, but with their wives on the weekends.

"Excuse me." She stepped up on the porch. "Do you know if Jax is inside?"

"No." Jax leaned forward, pushing his head and shoulders out of the dark. "He's right here."

"Ah." A little embarrassed, Cecelia drifted to within a few feet of him. "I hope I'm not intruding."

"Depends."

"On?"

"On why you're here. Have a seat." He motioned to the empty space on the bench beside him.

She moved to sit, but then backed up, quickly deciding sitting close to him seemed a bad idea. Simply because it was too enticing. "No, I won't take up your evening. I just wanted to...that is..." She trailed off, her words becoming choppy, directionless, like her thoughts. She moistened her lips. Why was this suddenly so hard? "I wanted to thank you again for chasing away the bear."

"You thanked me once or twice the other day. That's enough."

"I just felt I hadn't…I had to get past the shock, and I wanted to make sure you knew I knew you took a great risk. I'm grateful beyond words."

"I'm glad I was there."

He didn't sound annoyed or dismissive. Cecelia did, however, detect a slight hint of aloofness. There was a definite distance between them. "Have I somehow offended you, Jax? Or did I do something wrong?" Had she broken some Cowboy Code of Conduct, been too rough with her horse?

"No. What makes you ask that?"

Cecelia felt dangerous emotions stirring, stretching to wakefulness like a cat coming out of a nap. A tenderness. A warmth. Something like friendship, and she winced. Now that she was here, she wondered over her foolishness. She didn't care what Jax thought. "Nothing, I just wanted to make sure I hadn't offended you or done something wrong on the job. I'll see you in the morning."

She spun and hurried down the steps, away from the bunkhouse. Oddly, she halfway expected him to call out, stop her, continue the conversation. When he did, something in her chest jolted.

"I figured it out."

She stopped but didn't turn. Instead, she mulled over this sensation bubbling up in her like butterflies taking flight. "What?"

"It bothered me a lot when I said I could love from a distance. And you asked why that was bad."

She turned, curious. "And."

"If you love from a distance, it means you're afraid. And there's a scripture that says He hasn't given a spirit of fear, but of power, love, and a sound mind."

She honestly tried to understand what he was saying but couldn't. She inclined her head, waiting for a better explanation.

Jax rose and walked to the edge of the porch. He studied her for a moment, wrestling, she could tell, with what more to say. He dropped the remainder of his cigarette and crushed it with the toe of his boot. "Faith or fear. I can't have both. But I have to be wise, too. And sometimes that means hard choices."

A LITTLE WHILE later in the dorm, Cecelia sat on her cot, mindlessly combing her hair. The room was quiet. Most of the girls were asleep. A few were reading books or Bibles by frail lamp light. Above her, Virginia peered down from the perch of the upper berth.

"You're lookin' kinda dreamy eyed."

Cecelia heard the humor in the girl's voice but didn't look up. "Just tired."

The bed shook and squeaked, and momentarily, Virginia was seated beside Cecelia, brown eyes ever wide and curious as she worked her long, dark hair into a single braid for sleep. "I got me a feelin' you're thinkin' about a fella."

Cecelia paused the brush. Where exactly had her thoughts been? "I was thinking about Jax." She straightened. "I mean, I think I offended him somehow, but I don't know what I've done." Worse, why did she care? Why couldn't she just dismiss him from her mind?

Virginia's fingers slowed. She tilted her head, but Cecelia didn't look at her. "Why don't ya just ask him?"

"I did." And his answer had been aloof, most likely honest, but unfathomable. *Faith or fear. I can't have both. But I have to be wise, too. And sometimes that means hard choices.*

She couldn't begin to understand what he was saying. But mostly what bothered her now was her reaction to him.

Why had she gone to the bunkhouse? Because Jax, Virginia, Miss Sally—these people were like quicksand. Sucking her in…just look how she was ruminating on the man now. He was such a puzzle.

Worse, here she was discussing him with Virginia. The realization jolted her.

"And what did he say?"

Cecelia swung her gaze to Virginia, horrified she'd let the girl—or anyone else—past her walls. "I'm going to bed now."

"Oh." Virginia's brow rose, then dipped suddenly. "Sure thing." Her braid unfinished, she rose and climbed back into her bed.

Frustrated and sad, Cecelia did the same thing. As the last lamp in the dorm faded, she whispered, "I—I'm sorry, Virginia. That was rude."

A tense silence passed in the darkness before Virginia finally responded. "I forgive you. You sleep tight."

JAX REACHED across the desk and handed the ledger to Miss Sally. Chewing on a pencil, she studied the pages quietly. He sat down and waited for her thoughts. All the numbers looked good. Other ranchers in the area would kill for half the yield the Burning Dress was accomplishing.

"How's she doing?"

Jax blinked. "Beg pardon?"

"Cecelia." She laid the pencil down and looked at him. "There was a window there, I thought she was making a little progress."

He squirmed at the question. Though he wasn't quite sure why. Something about Miss Sally's gaze boring into him, piercing, like she already knew what he was thinking. He scratched his neck at his collar. "Uh, well, she's a fine hand." What did Cecelia have to do with the reports? And why was Miss Sally asking *him*?

"I just happened to notice, if I didn't see her with Virginia, I saw her with you."

Jax couldn't read the tone in her voice. "I'm not sure I get your meanin'."

"I thought she might be coming around. Making some friends...but the last few days...she's not as talkative at dinner. I'd say purposely trying to put distance between herself and others."

He ran a hand through his hair and wondered about the other night, when she'd come to the bunkhouse. She'd left all of a sudden, like a notion had struck her. Like maybe she'd recognized some walls were breaking down. Maybe *hers* were, and Jax had gone and tossed up some of his own. As he had to. Didn't he? Surely, he had to be careful with his heart.

Perfect love casts out fear...be wise as serpents, harmless as doves. The scriptures collided in his head.

"I'm sorry." She sighed and leaned back. "You didn't take her to raise."

"No, ma'am."

Still, that gaze. Like she knew something.

"She's a tough one. Needs to believe in people again, let go of her fear, or she'll never heal, never forgive." Her eyebrow ticked up. "Doesn't sound like anyone we know, does it?"

A sliver of irritation pricked his heart. Miss Sally was—

"Meddling. I am meddling in your affairs, Jax. I'm sorry. Forgiveness, though, frees a soul to live with joy and peace."

"Yes, ma'am. I don't disagree."

"And you don't want to discuss it. I overstep. Again, I'm sorry. You've been nothing but a blessing to the Burning Dress, but if you ever feel you need to go back to the Bar T—"

"No, ma'am. That bridge is burnt."

"I think he lit one end of it, but you lit the other." After a moment of awkward silence, she exhaled heavily. "So, let's talk about these reports."

WHEN JAX LEFT, Sally laced her fingers together on her desk and stared up at heaven. "Two of the toughest ones You've ever sent me, Lord." Her heart was heavy over Jax and Cecelia's stubborn refusal to acknowledge their pain. "The problem is, they think they're fine. They both think burying their bitterness is the same thing as forgiveness. And they're really just scared children." She drummed her fingers on the desk. "Until they deal with their hurts, Lord, neither one can live the life You want for them…" She trailed off, irritated with Jax and Cecelia. "Fear. They're bound up in fear and moving like molasses."

Behold, I am the Lord, the God of all flesh: is there anything too hard for me?

The scripture chastised Sally and she sighed, frustrated with herself now. "I'm sorry for my impatience, Lord. Getting ahead of You again. You'd think after all these years, patience would be one of my virtues."

A good-natured chuckle echoed down from heaven, warming Sally's heart.

CHAPTER ELEVEN

When Miss Sally announced the news at dinner that there would be a bonfire this evening, everyone looked up and cheered, except Virginia. Cecelia noticed and wrestled with whether she should be a busybody and ask if the girl was all right.

When she had finally decided she would venture the question, Virginia rose to her feet. "I'll see y'all later." She slipped away, leaving Cecelia and Wilhelma to exchange troubled glances.

"She's all right," Miss Sally said, reaching for her water. A smile played on her lips as she drained the glass. "And I'll see you two at the bonfire." With that, she slipped away as well.

Curiosity got the better of Cecelia and she finished her dinner quickly, as did Wilhelma. Shortly, they were outside with a growing crowd of female ranch hands.

The last of the sun had faded, leaving only a faint

hint of lavender sky, quickly giving way to a rising tide of black velvet. In moments, it was strewn with twinkling diamonds. The fire popped and hissed. A cool breeze off the mountains chilled the July night and Cecelia moved a few steps closer to the flames. As she rubbed her arms for circulation, Miss Sally stepped out of the darkness and took center stage.

"Good evening, ladies, thank you for joining us for a very special event." She laced her fingers in front of her and surveyed the crowd, as if making sure she had each and every woman's attention. Then she spoke. "Salvation, freedom, a relationship with our Lord. As I've told you all so many times before, He"—she pointed at the sky for emphasis—"He opens up the doors to a wonderful, blessed, abundant life. Tonight, I am so pleased to not only tell you that another one of the Burning Dress girls has become the bride of Christ, but she has special plans for her earthly gown." She turned to the shadows. "Virginia."

Cecelia sucked in a joyful gasp as Virginia, holding her wedding dress across her outstretched arms, walked from the darkness to stand beside Miss Sally. The woman nodded a go-ahead, and Virginia swallowed. "A month back, I told Cecelia there what brought me to Burning Dress. Most of y'all know I got drunk and my little girl wandered off and drowned in the crik." She stopped, her throat moving up and down. After several awkward seconds, she sniffed and carried on. "My husband, he—he didn't beat me or, or even scream at me. Just put me on the train, and I wound up here—"

She screwed her face up into a pinch of muscles, fighting for emotional control. She licked her lips and tried again. "He sent me here, not to the law, not to my people, He sent me to a place where I might have a chance to forgive myself. Miss Sally has told me over and over how much Jesus loves me. That once I ask Him to forgive me, why, He wouldn't even remember my sin." Her teary eyes landed on Cecelia. "Then I confessed my sin to someone who don't know me half as well as Jesus, and she—she forgave me. Still wanted to be my friend—" Virginia choked up, wrestled again for control of her voice.

Cecelia was astonished at the lump in her own throat. Yes, she did want to be Virginia's friend, and she smiled at the girl, hoping she could see the gesture in the fire's wavering light.

"Well, what she did made it…believable," Virginia continued. "Knowing how much more Jesus loves me —so much that He let them nail Him to a cross, to pay the price for my sins." Tears broke free and streamed down the girl's cheeks. "He loves me. He forgives me. And He is my Lord now." She raised the gown a little higher. "I've been thinking about Cara Newman losing her baby." Virginia glanced down at the wedding dress she held. "Instead of burning this thing, I want to make gowns out of it…for little angels to be buried in."

A stunned, beautiful silence hovered over the crowd. Except for the sniffles. And then Cecelia realized her cheeks were wet, too.

JAX NOTED that every Friday when the fiddle came out, Cecelia skedaddled out of the room. He swirled the punch in his glass and wondered if she'd do the same tonight. Watching her now, playing checkers with Virginia, he thought something was decidedly different about her.

Same slim figure in a simple blue dress, a glimmering wave of auburn silk cascading around her shoulders. She leaned into the board, studying her next move, but she and Virginia kept exchanging friendly glances filled with mirth, whispering giggly secrets, looking up to share their thoughts with Wilhelma, all of them bursting into laughter like little girls.

The three of them were a group. Real friendships had formed—much as Cecelia had most likely protested.

Her no-doubt grudging surrender made him smile. *Not so easy to love from a distance, is it, Cecilia?* And he wondered if he would have lost the bet about the turtle shell versus the eggshell.

Once again, Baxter picked up his fiddle, and the screeching, disjointed moans of a tuning fiddle signaled to the room that dancing was about to start. The mood in the room shifted, lightened even more, and Jax found it gave him an idea. No, truthfully, it gave him the courage—*foolishness?*—to follow through on something that had crossed his mind more than once.

Wise or not, Lord, I'm gonna dance with that girl one time. Just one time.

Cecelia rose, about to make her escape from the table, when Jax stepped into her path. He greeted all three of the girls with a dip of his head and his most winning smile. "Ladies, I expect to dance with each of you this evening." Blushes and smirks bloomed on Virginia and Wilhelma's faces. Cecelia stiffened up like a corpse.

Virginia tagged him on the sleeve. "I reckon you'd best start with Cecelia there before she bolts for the door."

Cecelia turned beet red, and murder entered those haunting, green eyes. Jax threw back his head and laughed, and Baxter obliged with the slow-moving and romantic *Annie Laurie*. He offered his hand to Cecelia. "I don't think you can get out of this."

Virginia frowned and nodded at her. Cecelia flicked her gaze to Wilhelma, who was less subtle. "Don't be *shtupid*. He's a fine dancer."

AND SOMEHOW CECELIA found herself on the dance floor, one hand in Jax's hand, one hand on his shoulder, his arm around her waist. Stunning blue eyes, the handsome, chiseled face, and beaming white smile tried working their charm on her. She swallowed and looked out at the other dancers, a total of five couples. She would have sworn everyone in the room could hear the hammering of her heart.

Good grief, what is the matter with me? I feel as if I've never danced with a man before...

"Cecelia..."

She looked up into a face she found so easy to like.

"Breathe," he said softly as they box-stepped. "And relax. It's just a dance. Just one dance."

He added the last with a husky catch in his tone, and she felt his breath on her forehead. Butterflies burst to life in her stomach, but his last statement echoed in her head. "Why just one?"

For a moment, his gaze stayed on her, then he blinked and looked out over the dancers. And he didn't answer. Puzzled, she let him lead her, twirl her once, and bring her back close to him for the next several steps. She caught the clean scent of oatmeal soap, lilac water, and leather. Lean, solid muscles in his shoulder flexing beneath her fingers made them tingle.

She realized she was falling down a rabbit hole of attraction.

She took a deep breath, exhaled slowly. *Don't lose your head to the Queen of Hearts, Cecelia.*

He stared down into the space between them and sighed. "Reckon 'cause I know better than to repeat certain mistakes."

What? Cecelia really was befuddled now. She'd lost her train of thought, and it came back together grudgingly. Just one dance, he'd said. "Are you saying this dance is a mistake? We can end—" She started to walk away, but he squeezed her hand tighter and pulled her close again, to the point she rested her free hand on his chest to keep the distance appropriate, but still their bodies collided. "I don't understand," she whispered, looking up into eyes that both kissed her soul and terrified her. She could feel his breath on her face, his heart pounding beneath her fingers, the warmth of his hand holding hers. Every sense in her body lit up as if hit by lightning. "Never mind...I think I do."

She wiggled a little freer of him and he let her go. The more appropriate space between them did nothing to stop her racing pulse. He cocked his head to the side and pursed his lips, as if accepting the change. "What did you say you did before you came to Burning Dress?"

"Before I was a wife, I was a teacher. Before that, I grew up on a farm."

"A teacher, huh? What did you teach?"

The soulful strains of Baxter's fiddle filled the room with gentle weeping. The song was such a beautiful, mournful, gushing declaration of love. Did Annie Laurie ever know how blessed she was to be loved by a man who would die for her? Looking into Jax's eyes, Cecelia could almost weep with the longing to know love like that. She cleared her throat. "French and German."

"You speak two languages?"

"Three." She smirked at the obvious math. "You're forgetting English."

He chuckled. "Three. Why aren't you teaching, then, instead of working as a ranch hand?"

"Partly, I think, because Miss Sally didn't need a teacher and she didn't want me doing something I already know how to do." He nodded broadly, as if he'd forgotten some mysterious, obvious goal of Burning Dress. "And, I have to admit," she continued, "I don't like teaching. I found it…restrictive. Not to mention a political minefield with emotionally draining parents." Baxter missed a note, but no one seemed to notice. "Tell me about you. Have you always been a cowboy?"

"Yes, ma'am. Born to it. My father owns a ranch."

"How did you wind up at the Bar T?" She bit her lip. "Pardon me if that is too personal."

Jax lowered his head, as if planning his answer. "The Bar T is a good spread. I knew I could help make it bigger and better. And I did."

"Oh, then you had a falling out with Mr. Taylor?"

"Yeah."

"The Burning Dress is quite successful. Is that due to your management?"

He chuckled. "Burning Dress has always done well under Miss Sally. She is a blessed and highly favored rancher. I've learned from her, to be honest."

The fiddle faded and the dance was done. Their feet stopped moving, but they held each other's gazes, still entwined in each other's arms. Cecelia didn't want to stop dancing and the realization frightened her. Jax gave her a soft, half-smile and stepped away from her with a nod. "You know, I think I'll turn in. Apologize to Virginia and Wilhelma for me, if you would?"

"Certainly."

"And thank you for the dance."

His departure left her cold, as if she'd stepped outside on a winter's day. *What's happening to me?* she wondered. She laid a hand on her breast, surprised at the pain she felt and wished she'd never given in to the one dance.

CHAPTER TWELVE

Cecelia had been doing all right watching everyone go to town on Saturdays, and could have gone two weeks ago, but a cow stuck in a bog had required her assistance. The next Saturday, a hail-storm had waylaid the planned trip. Finally, today, her chance to get off the ranch rolled around—excitement woke her up early. She rode into Hell's Half-Acre with several girls, including Miss Sally, Maria, Molly, Virginia, and Wilhelma.

After purchasing some personal items in the mercantile and storing them in the wagon, she politely declined a lunch invitation. She wanted to wander the town, explore a little, buy a newspaper, and maybe sit in the shade of a cottonwood to read it. Her ultimate goal: to be alone for a spell. The disappointment she'd seen in their eyes, especially Virginia's, had nearly changed her mind.

But the day was sunny. A pleasant, gentle breeze stirred the branches in the cedars on the edge of town, and the traffic was light on the boardwalk. So, she walked, taking in Hell's Half-Acre. Dusty and weathered, but industrious. The businesses, from the dress shop to the bakery to the bank, were busy. She turned around when she saw the saloon. She'd received a few bold hat-tips from passing cowboys and didn't want to accidentally put herself in the wrong part of town.

One cowboy swaggered past her, a tall fella with shaggy hair and dirt defining the lines around his eyes. He grinned broadly, tipped his hat, but walked on, craning his neck for a few more steps. Cecelia smiled, but not at him. At the memory of Jax, of being in his arms last night. The smile almost instantly faded into a troubled frown. He'd said just one dance. And she'd agreed, that was best. She didn't know his reasons, but she was quite clear on hers. Like everyone else at the Burning Dress, Jax was quicksand.

She spotted a dress in the window of the dress shop and let it distract her. A lovely shade of indigo with a full skirt, broad bustle, and white lace across the bodice and cuffs, she wondered if she'd ever have cause again to dress for a party.

I can't be a cowboy my whole life, enjoyable as it is. This thought was followed immediately, however, by the question, *Why not?*

"Pretty dress for a pretty gal."

Cecelia turned at the deep, gravelly voice. A tall, slender cowboy winked at her. Pale blue eyes contrasted noticeably with his darkly tanned, pockmarked face. He grinned, showing yellowed, unkempt teeth.

Cecelia ducked her head. "Thank you," was all she could think to say as she moved to charge past him.

To her shock, he grabbed her arm. "You're new in town. I saw you on Miss Sally's wagon."

Anger got the better of her judgment and she snatched her arm free. "I beg your pardon. How dare you touch me?"

Again, she attempted to rush past him, but this time he stepped in front of her, resting a hand on the bullwhip at his side. "Don't take offense, ma'am. That was a sincere compliment. You're 'bout the prettiest thing I've seen since I come to Hell's Half-Acre."

He towered over her and she took a step back. "Sir, sincere or not, your advances are unwanted. Now, please, get out of my way."

"You ready for that sarsaparilla, Miss Cecelia?" Jax's voice came from behind the man and he spun. "I'm sure you've got some place to be, Woodward." Jax was leaning on the doorframe of the dress shop, arms folded casually across his chest, his black hat resting in his left hand. "Some job to do for Taylor so he can pat you on the back."

Woodward's gaze darted back and forth between him and Cecelia, but she saw the thinly veiled fury.

Jax pushed off the doorway and extended his hand. "Ma'am."

Cecelia moistened her lips, stepped past Woodward, and slipped her fingers into Jax's. His grasp raised goosebumps on her skin. Something menacing glinted in Woodward's eyes as he followed her movement, but he blinked it away and gave her a cold smile. Touching the brim of his hat, he nodded to her. "Till next time, ma'am."

Cecelia did not respond as the man strode on without a look back. She waited until he was several yards away before she breathed. Then she, and apparently Jax, realized at the same moment they were still holding hands. They released each other as if the temperature in their fingers had suddenly soared.

Cecelia swallowed and started walking. "Thank you. Did I recognize him?"

"I don't know." Fanning his hat about nervously, Jax fell into step beside her, and the pair strolled down the boardwalk. "Did he look familiar?"

"Maybe. Is he the one you tangled with just after the stampede?"

"Yep."

She digested the news for a moment before she spoke again. "I don't like the way he was looking at me. I hope I never run into him out on the range."

"If you do, don't trust him. He's roughed up a couple of the girls at Sam's Place."

Several more steps passed in silence before Cecelia spoke. She could still feel the gentle, warm pressure of his fingers on hers, but tried not to think about it. "Just in case I wasn't effusive enough, thank you. You have a penchant for showing up when I'm in need."

Jax shrugged. "He wouldn't have done much here on the street other than be a nuisance."

Cecelia knew he was right, but still, the man gave

her the shivers. She cut her eyes at Jax and caught him looking at her. He quickly snatched his gaze elsewhere. As they strolled, he chewed on his lip, ran his tongue over his teeth, then finally shrugged. "The gal I was infatuated with, Pauline, her goal was to get close to my pa. He has a lot of money."

"Do you mean she used you?"

"Like a gold-plated footstool."

"That's cold." Not as cold as William's verbal abuse, but cold just the same. "Where is she now?"

"She was arrested and extradited to France. For embezzlement. A French politician."

"My, she was a busy girl. What of your father? How did he—*why* did he…?" She faded off, chiding herself for her curiosity but touched by the sadness in Jax's face.

He huffed a big sigh and rubbed his neck, as if the muscles had tightened up suddenly. "He went behind my back. I found out they were engaged before she'd even broken off anything with me. As you might imagine, my pa and me, we don't talk much anymore."

"I'm sorry." And she was. She could see that Jax felt the betrayals deeply.

"Worst thing about it was, I let her distract me from my faith. She made a fool of me, and I dealt with it by turning my back on God and spending too much time in the saloon."

"How did you…" She struggled with the words. "How did you right yourself after something like that?"

He took several seconds to answer. Cecelia didn't

push. "Miss Sally. She made it her mission to point me back to true North."

"True North? The Bible," she muttered, comprehending at least this much.

"The One who brings joy and peace into my life. I had it. I let Pauline and Pa take it from me. Won't happen again."

He sounded vaguely as if he was accusing Cecelia of trying. Of course, she wasn't. She was a little curious, however, about a connection with God that could bring both joy and peace.

"Anyway…" He shrugged. "In the past now. What about you?"

"What about me?"

He shrugged again. "Just thought you, I mean, if you wanted to talk…"

"All of us at the ranch. We all have an injury, don't we?"

"I believe so."

She didn't want to tell him hers. Yet, something about Jax pulled it from her. "When my husband began to suspect I couldn't give him a child, he… became cruel. Verbally abusive. Explained in detail how worthless, what a failure, I was to him as a wife, and what a drain I was on his finances. When the doctor confirmed the suspicion, he divorced me." *Long story short.*

Jax made a *tsking* sound. "Clearly, he was a special kind of stupid."

Cecelia snorted and immediately pressed a hand

to her mouth to hold back any similar unladylike sounds. "I wouldn't argue."

"I'm sorry. No one should say things like that to anyone. Especially when they're not true."

She watched the play of emotions across his handsome face, tightening the muscles in his cheeks. Had he said cruel things, too? Had his father said them to him?

"William had a very detailed plan for his life," she explained. "He just never bothered to share it with me. And when I became an obstacle to that plan, he was done. William was nothing if not decisive."

"No shades of gray with him."

"None."

"Sometimes it would be good to be that clear on things, I guess."

Her pace slowed. "It was jarring. In a span of a few months, I went from being treated like a human being to rubbish set out on the curb." She blinked. "Hence, back to our discussion of loving from a distance. I say it's a safer, better way to live. Best to avoid the pain altogether."

"Yeah. Maybe. I don't know." Frowning, he dropped his gaze to the boardwalk. "I think you just have to be real intentional with who you distance yourself from and why."

Cecelia, again, was at a loss to understand what was happening behind the foreman's hypnotic blue eyes. When he looked at her with almost a pained expression, her confused train of thought came apart.

"You, uh, you don't know the Lord, do you?"

Cecelia was a bit offended by the question. "We are not exactly on a first-name basis."

He motioned weakly to the shingle hanging up ahead for Lou's Café. "I am, uh, happy to buy you that sarsaparilla for real, if you're inclined."

The invitation sounded too obligatory. She decided to practice a little self-discipline, painful as it was. "Thank you, but some other time."

It seemed prudent to stick with the idea of loving from a distance—not that love was involved here at all. Merely self-preservation. Mitigating the risks.

"Well, all right then, I'll see you back at the ranch." He waved with his hat and pulled open the screen door, disappearing inside.

Alone on the boardwalk, Cecelia wondered why she was annoyed. If she understood the cryptic conversation they'd just had, Jax wanted some distance from Cecelia. Did it have to do with his question regarding religion? Considering she wanted the same distance, why was she put out?

She kicked at a nail in the boardwalk and turned her irritation on herself. *This is why you don't talk. This is why you don't ask questions, get details. This fondness for these people has to stop with Virginia. Even one dance with him was one dance too many.*

She glanced at the café door and tried to ignore the sadness spreading over her like a shadow. Not much of a way to live, perhaps, but look at the turmoil she was already tangled in. *It has to stop here.*

Determined, she headed back toward Miss Sally and the wagon.

JAX HAD NEVER BEEN MUCH GIVEN to a sweet tooth, but something about a good, flavorful sarsaparilla sure pulled his trigger. Especially when it was cold. Lou's Café in town kept the bottles in the spring out back. He wouldn't have minded sharing one with Cecelia, but at the same time was glad she'd declined the invitation. He reminded himself once more to keep her at a distance. He'd liked holding her hand a little too much. And the dance last night...her in his arms. It would be a long time before he forgot the feel of her, or the gentle scent of rose water in her hair, her hesitant smile, a mouth made for kissing...

Fool, he scolded.

With a sigh, he sat down on the bench outside Lou's, pulled the cork, and took a long, cool, satisfying swig. Slowly enjoying the drink, however, only gave him time for his mind to ponder Cecelia, and some of the ideas he'd been swatting at lately like flies.

Forgiveness. Fear. Love.

She wasn't a Believer, and that was reason enough to avoid her like the plague. But was it the *real* reason?

A nagging worry, like a hag's bony finger, kept poking at him, pushing him to consider how he really felt about Pauline Lautrec's lying, her facade of love...and his father's betrayal. Maybe Jax hadn't *forgiven* them, per se. Maybe he had buried his pain simply to avoid dealing with it. And maybe that was a cowardly way of veering around touchy emotions, not saying things that should be said, not risking any actual healing or pursuing authentic relationships.

That was the thing that bothered him about being around Cecelia. When she was beside him as they worked, it was a comfortable thing like worn boots. When they danced, she felt like she was made for his arms. She lit a fire in him, but it didn't fog his brain the way Pauline had...

He took a sip and exhaled softly, annoyed with the assessment.

A shadow fell across him as a deep, throaty laugh drained off what little joy he had in the sarsaparilla. "Enjoying your lady's drink?"

Woodward. The drink soured in Jax's mouth. Holding back a scowl—barely—he looked up. "I was. You're tampin' it down some."

Woodward chuckled and leaned back on the porch rail, resting one boot in its scrolling woodwork and a hand on the ever-present whip. "Where's that pretty gal you were with earlier?"

Fire kindled in Jax's chest. "I can't believe you think that's any of your business."

Spurs jangled and another man from the Bar T meandered up. Wiry, blond, and in need of a bath, he was cleaning his nails with a pocketknife and chuckling as well. Jax knew him. A mean-spirited Irishman named Chauncey.

Woodward tagged Chauncey lightly in the ribs. "I reckon workin' with a bunch of women could soften a man's pallet for a harder drink." Both men laughed, but then Woodward cut his gaze back to Jax. "I heard you used to frequent the saloon on a right regular basis."

A snippet of a memory slammed into Jax like a train. "Not anymore." Though hazy, the drunken fistfight with his father was one of the most degrading moments in his life. That he'd sunk so low. Over a woman. And the vicious accusations they'd both spat had drawn as much blood as the punches. Partly because of the truth behind them. At least the shameful scene had put an abrupt end to Jax's drinking. "Nothin' good comes from hanging around alcohol. Look at you."

"Least I ride with men. And Mr. Taylor says I'm the best foreman he's ever had. Why, he almost treats me like a son."

Jax should have ignored the deliberate poke, but Woodward made it so easy to snarl right back. Slowly, he stood up. "I guess a mongrel like you would be glad to have a daddy. Any daddy." Woodward's lips stretched out into a thin, angry line. Jax corked his sarsaparilla and set it on the bench. "And those women I ride with were back in the saddle the next day after you tried to scare 'em off. I'd say the wrong ranch is wearing the petticoats."

Woodward launched to his feet. "I ought to—"

"Know when you're licked. But I can do it again, if need be."

Woodward, clenching his jaw, hands curled into tight fists, shook his head. "I owe you one, that's for sure. But I can't. Not yet." Woodward wheeled away from Jax and stomped off in a hurry, like he might change his mind and make a huge mistake.

But Chauncey remained.

The Irishman was grinning like a mischievous leprechaun. "I hear those gals are pretty hard workin'." He folded the knife and put it away. "Go all day...and then all night."

The town of curious gossips had spread all kinds of rumors about the Burning Dress, but no one had ever dared voice anything malicious directly to Jax or Miss Sally's face. Insulting a woman, especially all those good hands back at the ranch, was something he just couldn't let pass. He only wished Chauncey wasn't acting as a proxy for Woodward, doing the man's dirty work to keep him out of trouble with Taylor. Well, so be it.

He stepped up to Chauncey. They were of equal height, but Jax was heavier. "Taylor didn't tell you boys to stand down like I asked, did he?" It wasn't a question.

A slimy, sideways grin pasted itself on the cowhand's mouth, dirt-filled creases deepening around his eyes. "Not in precise language, no." He sucked on his teeth for a second. "Woodward seems to have taken the order to heart, but with a bit of a loophole." His grin widened. "Me."

Chauncey's fist struck out like a lightning bolt, fast and painful, the right hook slamming into Jax's mouth. Caught off guard, but only for an instant, he ignored the stars in his eyes and the throb in his lips, raised his arm to ward off the next punch, and threw his own. He hammered Chauncey with a powerful uppercut so hard the Irishman's teeth clacked together.

Chauncey staggered back but shook it off and came for Jax in the next breath, throwing a clumsy haymaker. It connected, but barely delivered a sting. Stepping in close, Jax jabbed Chauncey in the gut, right in the breadbasket. The wind *ooophed* out of him in a great exhalation and he doubled over, gasping for a breath.

"That is enough, boys." Sam Hain stepped up on the boardwalk, casually swinging a walking cane, as if he couldn't be more bored by yet another street brawl in Hell's Half-Acre. Jax and Chauncey separated with sheepish—and, in Chauncey's case—sick, expressions, like two first graders caught tussling by the teacher.

"Jax, I don't think Sall—Miss Sally would want you fighting with this bloody hooligan." He cut his eyes to a huffing, winded Chauncey who was holding his midsection. Hain pointed his cane at him. "This is over."

The Bar T hand apparently took offense at the order or the imperial tone. Maybe both. Straightening, he cursed and spat blood at Hain's feet. "Ye're no English lord—"

Moving with the speed of a rattler, Hain was suddenly nose-to-nose with Chauncey. "I am your worst nightmare," he hissed. "If you do not do exactly as I say, I will invade your dreams and make you wet your bed like an infant. I will give you nightmares so severe you'll think your brain is crawling with maggots."

The two men glared at each other, but the anger in Chauncey's eyes quickly changed to confused, undeniable fear, as if he were seeing into the fires of hell, and he backed away, nearly stumbling over his own feet. He glanced at Jax, swiped his hat from the ground, and hurried down the boardwalk, breaking into a run after three wild, staggering steps.

Jax swallowed and looked over at Hain. He wasn't afraid of the man, but he was befuddled by Chauncey's reaction. How did he, what did he—?

"You're bleeding." Hain whipped a silk handkerchief from his pocket and handed it to Jax, who absently pressed it to his mouth. "Does this tiff indicate Taylor and his men have been giving you trouble?"

"Some. Seems to be upping the ante here lately, though. I guess that's my fault."

"It's Woodward. He's exploiting the rift between you and Quitman. He's the devil at the Bar T." Hain turned to face Jax. A darkness burned in the man's eyes that chilled him to the bone. "And I would know." His gaze drifted down the boardwalk to the departing cowboy. "But I can't have those boys threatening the Burning Dress. I'll have to speak with them." Hain sounded like a teacher eager to discipline some unruly students. But suddenly the fire in his gaze cooled and his countenance changed, lightened, and he touched his cravat, as if making sure it was still knotted perfectly. "Please give Miss Sally my regards." He waved with the handle of his cane. "Good day."

CHAPTER THIRTEEN

Two days passed in which Jax couldn't let go of Hain's threat or whatever it was he'd promised to the Bar T boys. He wondered repeatedly whether to mention it to Miss Sally or not. The idea had been growing on him, even though it struck him a little like gossip. After praying about it, however, the sense of urgency actually increased, deciding for him.

Miss Sally was sitting at her desk studying her Bible, but waved him in nonetheless when he knocked. "What can I do for you, Jax?" She gently closed the book and leaned back in her chair, giving the impression that he had all of her attention. "How's your lip?"

He had mumbled an excuse the other day, not a lie, but not the truth, and that hadn't sat well with him, either. "Um…" He touched his mouth gingerly, unsure of where to start. He dragged off his hat and sat down. "I didn't do this on the ranch, like I implied. I had words in town the other day with Woodward and that fella Chauncey."

"Woodward. He's starting to become a nuisance."

"Yes, ma'am. Hain said almost the same thing."

"Sam was there?"

Jax would have to have been blind to miss the light in her eyes or the tenderness in her voice. "He saw most of it. Um..." He chided himself for hemming and hawing as he slid to the edge of his seat. "I asked Taylor to rein in Woodward. According to Chauncey, though...well, Woodward is delegating his dirty work."

"Delegating? So, you're thinking the Bar T boys are going to keep plaguing us, huh? And the mighty Quitman Taylor is giving the orders...or not? What are you saying?"

"I think Woodward may be taking some broad liberties with what Taylor is telling him to do, but Taylor isn't completely unaware."

I'll have to speak with them.

Why did Hain's words have the ring of a threat? He tugged on his ear, buying a moment to think.

"What is it, Jax? What do you really want to say?"

"I'm not sure. Hain—he threw the fear of God into Chauncey, the likes of which I've never seen. I mean, the man ran from town. Ran."

Miss Sally's face fell, tensed with obvious anxiety. "Did he threaten him?"

"Referring to the boys from the Bar T, he said he'd have to *speak with them.*" He shook his head, flustered.

"It's not what he said, it's the way he said it. I-I...I don't know. It's hard to explain. Hain seems..."

"Dangerous."

Jax would have said *ready to kill,* but held it back.

"He can be. Unfortunately. If you don't know how to handle him."

Jax studied the beautiful, middle-aged woman before him, with her long, silver braid, trim figure, unusual violet eyes. She was still a looker. Must have been something in her younger days. How many years had she known Hain? And why was she the only person in town not afraid of him? She was sure the only person in town he gave a flip about.

"You two go way back?" he ventured hesitantly, knowing full well it was none of his business.

She smiled a little wistfully. "You could say that."

Before either of them could say anything at all, Lowdy burst through the door, his eyes wide with fear, and his face looked as if he'd been stomped. Blood trickled from his nose, his right eye was swelling shut, a red stain contrasted jarringly with his white hair. "Miss Sally, we got us a problem." She and Jax leaped to their feet as the man rushed to her desk and leaned on it, as if he might collapse. "Them boys from the Bar T. They jumped us out at Salter's Crik. Said we were stealing their cattle. Those mavs were on our land, I swear it. I swear it—"

"It's all right." Miss Sally raised her hands, motioning for calm. "It's all right. Tell me what's happened."

"They took 'em. Knocked me in the head and took 'em."

"The cattle?" Jax asked.

"No." Lowdy swung his gaze wildly back and forth between Jax and Miss Sally. "No, the girls. They took Cecelia and Molly."

Cecelia? The world slipped out from beneath Jax's feet. The icy finger of fear shot up his spine, followed almost instantly by a growing flame of fury. "Do you know where they are?"

"No idea. They wouldn't go back to the Bar T, would they?"

Jax crammed his hat on his head. "I don't know, but that's where I'm gonna start. With Taylor."

"Jax." Miss Sally raised her hand to stop him. "I'm not sure you should go alone. Take Baxter or one of the other men with you. In the meantime, we'll all be getting saddled up and come along right behind you."

JAX PULLED Nickels to a stop and pinched sweat from his upper lip as he surveyed the thick, swaying grass. Miles of it, and a thousand rolling hills between the Burning Dress and the Bar T. *Lord, I'm at a loss. I have no peace about going there. Woodward is pulling his own plans together...*

"Whacha thinkin'?" Baxter asked from beside him. An older fella, he'd been with the Burning Dress the longest of anyone.

"That Taylor don't really have control of Woodward. He's a loose cannon."

"And?"

And...What, Lord? Something I should— He snapped his fingers. "There's an old line shack 'bout a mile from here. I found a Cheyenne girl there a while back who'd been roughed up by somebody."

"I ain't following ya."

And Jax knew. "It'd be a good place to hide certain activities. Or people."

"We could find out quick-like."

"Way ahead of ya."

SEVERAL HUNDRED YARDS from the old cabin, Jax and Baxter dismounted and crept quietly through the jungle of grass to the top of a hill overlooking the building. The old ranch hand was spry for his sixty years and kept up easily.

They peered down and Jax was only a little surprised to find that not only was the cabin occupied, someone had built a couple of outbuildings and a corral near it. Four horses were milling around, the Bar T brands in plain sight.

Baxter peered through the grass and hunkered down a little more. "Bet that's them."

"Jax?" a voice whispered from the grass.

He and Baxter spun, guns drawn, peering into the thick growth of buffalo grass. A flash of red, the sound of rustling, and a moment later, Molly's tear-streaked face emerged from the weeds.

Jax clutched her shoulder and forced her below the tops of the grass. "That hair of yours is like a beacon. Are you all right?"

She nodded furiously. "I'm fine, but they've still got Cecelia." Tears choked her voice.

Jax patted the air. "Hey, now, she's gonna be okay." He turned to Baxter. "Get her back to the ranch. Tell Miss Sally where I am."

"Don't have to tell me twice—" Baxter was turning to go when furious screams spewed forth from one of the outbuildings. The trio squatted lower and watched as Woodward wrestled Cecelia from the shadows of a shed and dragged her toward the cabin. Mollie strangled a cry. Cecelia was not going easily, giving the cowboy everything her slight frame had—kicking, punching, clawing, and digging in her heels.

Something inside Jax's chest twisted up tighter than rawhide strings when he saw her caught in Woodward's abusive hand. *Oh, God, give me the strength of Samson.* "Baxter, go, get help fast."

"What are you gonna do?"

"Whatever I have to. Hurry."

He and Molly disappeared in the grass like ghosts.

Jax checked the cartridges in his Colt.

Woodward, panting and sweating, managed to drag Cecelia inside the cabin and slam the door shut. Jax's heart hammered in his chest like a charging bull as he feared for her and grimly imagined the pain he was going to inflict on Woodward. First, though, he had to be smart. Busting in there, crazy with fury, without knowing who was where, could get Cecelia killed.

He holstered his Colt, stayed low, and scurried bent over through the grass, then along an old, dilapidated fence till he was about twenty feet from the cabin. She was still screaming, but she sounded ferociously angry, and Jax had to smile at her courage. *Keep fighting, Cecelia, I'm coming...*

The structure only had four small windows, one on each wall. He drew his gun again and quickly, quietly rushed to the back wall, pressing up flat against it. Inside, men laughed, and furniture scraped on the floor as Cecelia continued her fight.

"I DON'T WANT to have to hurt you," Woodward roared, holding on to Cecelia's shoulders and shaking her violently.

"Then let me go," she screamed back, trying with all her might to sound brave. Three other ranch hands stood behind Woodward, eyeing her like wolves cornering a rabbit. She was not brave. She was terrified.

"Now, I said we're gonna have a party, gal. You are going to entertain us this afternoon."

"But Molly got away. She'll go for help. Someone could be here any second." At least the two girls had accomplished that much against these men.

The cowboys laughed again, and Woodward

leered at her, dirt and razor stubble highlighting his weathered, scarred face. He ran his tongue over yellow teeth and grinned. "There ain't nobody out here for miles. She'll be starved to death before she sees her first steer."

Blind with fury and panic, Cecelia growled and clawed for his face. The action only brought down a stinging blow, knocking tears from her eyes and an involuntary moan from her throat. Her face burned, her ears rang. Woodward pulled her nose-to-nose with him and spoke in a calm, menacing tone. "I don't want to hurt you, but I will."

"You, in the cabin!"

Jax! The instant Cecelia heard Jax's voice, hope both blossomed in her heart and withered from fear. *He'll get himself killed...there are four of them.*

The men fell silent, drew their guns, and took up positions to peer out the small windows in the cabin. Woodward shoved Cecelia hard up against the back wall, held her by the throat, and drew his gun, too, pointing it at the door. "Jax, that you?"

"Let her—I mean, let those girls go before this turns bad."

"Sounds like he's pressed up against the wall," one of the cowboys said, trying to see out the dusty window. Considering the shack was built with eight- to ten-inch logs, Cecelia surmised Jax was safe...for the moment.

"Jax, we're a little busy right now." Woodward grinned at Cecelia. The look in his eyes raised goose-flesh on her arms. "He would try to spoil our fun now," he said under his breath, then louder, "You get outta here. We're fixing to have a little party with your *cowboy*." The other three joined him in mocking laughter.

"Ooooh, that's why you won't fight me," Jax taunted. "Gotta stick to little girls. And send drooling lackeys like Chauncey to handle your battles."

Chauncey shot Woodward a baleful glare. "Let me kill him. He ain't got Hain around now."

"Come on, Woodward," Jax goaded. "Why don't you come out here and fight something that don't wear petticoats? Something that weighs more than a hundred pounds soaking wet. A man."

"No," Woodward muttered, but he didn't sound firm. "Get outta here!" He looked at Chauncey. "Wait till he's running and then go—"

"You're a good little lap dog for the old man. You do exactly what he says. Till he ain't lookin'. Tell me: you won't fight me 'cause of his orders, or are you just afraid I'll beat the hound out of you again?"

"I ain't afraid of nothin'," Woodward growled loud and clear. "I'da fought you six times over, but Taylor told me not to touch you."

"Sounds like even he thinks I'll whip you again."

"You're just mad 'cause I took your job."

"I gave it away, you witless fool."

"Taylor says hiring me was the best thing he ever did for the Bar T. Bet he never said that to you."

"That right there ought to tell you how impaired his judgment is."

Woodward ground his teeth. His grip on Cecelia's

throat tightened, but she pawed at his hand and he relaxed his fingers.

What was Jax trying to do? Cecelia wondered. He needed to leave, go for help. She opened her mouth to scream those very words, but Jax called her name.

"Cecelia—" He stopped, as if choosing his words carefully. "You and Molly givin' them a good what-for in there?"

Was this a coy way of asking where the other girl was? "Molly got away," she cried.

Sneering, Woodward tightened the grip on her throat, squeezing, slowly, slowly. She slapped at his hand as her vision blurred. "Hold your tongue."

"Yeah, it would take four of Taylor's men to hold on to one of my hands."

"Shut your trap, Jax," Woodward snarled. "Or I'll snap this little girl's neck like a twig."

"Big man. Fighting little girls. But I promise you, Woodward, you belly-crawling, yellow coward, you hurt her, and I will kill you graveyard dead. You'll run, because that's what cowards do, but I will find you, God as my witness."

Woodward hammered the wall with Cecelia's head then released her. She stumbled and slithered to the floor, holding her head as pain rocketed through her skull. Two of the other cowboys chuckled, eyeing her with lascivious intent as she rubbed the goose egg already forming on her skull.

Chauncey, however, glared at Woodward. "He's baitin' ye. Let's just shoot him and then have the girl. It's gettin' late."

Cecelia sucked in her breath. *Oh, Jax, you and your awful, beautiful courage. It's going to get you killed.* "Jax, just go get help," she yelled, climbing to her feet. "There are too many of them."

Woodward half-turned on her. "He should run, if he knows what's good for him."

"You don't understand." Her head thundered so badly the pain whipped up a sickening wave of nausea. "He should run, yes. But he won't. And one of you is going to die."

"Come on, Woodward," Jax mocked. "Show me all the men at the Bar T aren't liars and cowards. Prove to me you have a spine."

For an instant, Cecelia thought she saw the slightest hint of doubt in Woodward's eyes, but then he spun around, shoved Chauncey out of the way, and flung open the front door. "I'll fight you, and this time I'll be ready for ya."

Cecelia heard movement outside. The men in the cabin scurried to the door, but Woodward raised his hand. "Everybody stay out of this. He's mine." He stepped down off the porch. The three cowboys, followed by Cecelia, filtered outside onto the porch to watch.

Jax stood about twenty feet away, boots squarely planted, gun drawn and pointed at Woodward. She couldn't help but admire him, his courage, his strength, his penchant for self-sacrifice. And something deep within her soul cried out to God. *Oh, Lord, please don't let him die, especially for me. I'm not worth it.*

The prayer caught her off guard, the way it had

bubbled up so naturally, as if some connection to God had been there in her heart all along. *Desperate times,* she thought absently. Yet, she couldn't stop another plea, *Lord, please, he's a good man.*

Woodward holstered his gun and started working his belt free. He did not remove the whip at his side, Cecelia noted.

"We settle this now—just you and me, Jax. I'm sick to death of hearing about your days as foreman at the Bar T. I'm gonna beat you so bad you'll be lucky to crawl back to the Burning Dress."

"You're fightin' ghosts, Woodward." Jax removed his gun belt as well, gently tossing his Colt a few feet away. "You ain't gonna measure up to me. You never will. And you'll never be like a son to him."

"Won't have to worry about it when you're dead."

"Big talk from a lily-livered lickspittle." He glanced up at the porch, his gaze passing over the cowboys, lingering on Cecelia. "Either way, she rides outta here safe and sound and untouched."

"Jax..." Cecelia pushed her way to the front, but what could she say? Things were in motion now. He couldn't walk away. Oh, God, how she wanted him to survive this. Fear choked her, smothered her with its heavy hand.

"I want you to know, Cecelia..." A slight smile twitched at the corner of his mouth, and his sapphire eyes glittered with warmth. "Turns out, I might be doing this for a little more than brotherly love."

CHAPTER FOURTEEN

Sally led Lowdy into the kitchen, where Maude dropped the potatoes she was peeling at the sight of her injured husband.

He tossed up a hand. "I'm all right, woman. Don't fuss over me."

Maude commenced to clucking over her husband like a hen, and Sally grinned at the pair as she set Lowdy down at the long kitchen table. "You take care of him, Maude. I've got riders to rustle up." She turned to go.

"What's happened?" Maude asked as she pressed a cloth to her husband's head.

"A little trouble with Taylor," Sally said over her shoulder. "But it will be all right. When you've got Lowdy squared away, please gather everyone in the house for prayer."

"Yes, ma'am."

Sally stormed toward the barn with a sense of heaviness hanging over her. "I've grown fond of those three, Lord, and I ask You to protect them. Give Your angels charge over them." Still, the sense of someone else in danger stalked her as she picked up her pace. Not *someone.*

Sam.

Please, keep him away from this situation, Father. He's run so far from You, I'm afraid one more thing... She shook her head, trying to clear it and loosen the knot strangling her throat. *Just, please don't let Satan give him an excuse—*

"Miss Sally?" Peering sideways at Sally, Virginia stepped down off the saddle shop's porch. She narrowed her wide eyes, evoking as serious a gaze as was possible for Virginia. "You look like you're a-feared of something awful."

Sally stopped and took a deep breath. "Not afraid." Or maybe that was it exactly. *Be anxious for nothing...*a still, small voice reminded her. "Concerned would be a better word. I want a good number of us to ride over to Taylor's..." No, that wasn't right. *But You'll show me where, Lord.* "Saddle up and come with us. Cecelia and Molly, and maybe Jax, are in trouble."

Virginia's expression changed to a stony, determined one, and her lips melted into a thin, angry line. "You just try to stop me."

NOBODY SAID the fight would be fair. As Woodward was slinging his gun belt to the ground, Jax dove in, head-butting the man in the chest and sending his carcass flying backward. He landed on his tail and Jax dove in again, swinging. Woodward swept Jax's legs, though, and dropped him to the ground. Both men scrambled to their feet, exchanging punches.

Jax jabbed, jabbed, jabbed Woodward in the face, snapping his head back. Blood gushed from the man's mouth. In spite of it, he managed to catch Jax in the jaw with a good strike. For a moment, he saw stars, tasted his own blood. He flailed blindly, connected with Woodward's ribs by good fortune, and the man backed up.

Jax gave no quarter and laid into him with a right cross and a left hook. Woodward was dazed, his punches were losing steam, and Jax thought the tide was turning in his favor.

He hammered the man with three more stout blows, and Woodward staggered back, then dropped to his knees. Jax had him on the ropes. He stepped in—

Cecelia screamed, and blinding, white-hot pain exploded in Jax's skull. He went down, cradling his head. He rolled on the ground, writhing, blind with the agony. Through a gray mist, he caught a glimpse of Chauncey slipping his .44 back into his holster.

"No," Woodward bellowed, flailing, lurching to his feet. "He's mine! Mine! Stay away from him." His voice warbled with rage. "Stay away from him!"

Get on your feet, boy...

"Jax, get up..." Cecelia's frightened plea cut through the fog. The only way she was getting out of here unharmed was if Jax went with her. Gritting his teeth, he gained his feet. Swaying, he raised his fists and tried to focus on Woodward. The cowboy launched toward him, raining blows on Jax.

He literally sucked them up, absorbed them, blocked a left hook, and by instinct stepped in with an uppercut. Again, Woodward staggered. Fire burned in Jax's brain. He used the pain to focus solely on hammering his opponent with blow after blow. Woodward tried to ward off the strikes and, at the same time, free the whip on his side. It unfurled, but he didn't have room to use it.

"Come on, Woodward," Chauncey taunted. "Cut his bloody ear off!"

Jax grabbed the whip, wrapped it around his forearm. He and Woodward scuffled furiously for control of it. Jax knew he couldn't let the man use it, not if he valued his eyes or the skin on his back.

He struck Woodward in the temple with everything in him. The man wavered with the blow, dazed for an instant. Jax reacted quickly, snatching the whip out of Woodward's hands and tossing it away. The cowboys moaned with disappointment.

Woodward growled like a wounded lion and threw punches wildly, viciously. He was getting tired and sloppy though, and Jax's confidence grew. He kept swinging. Blow after blow connected with Woodward's nose, his jaw, his mouth again. His face turned to a bloody mash, and finally he went down on his knees, gulping for air.

Mercifully, this was almost over as Jax was at the

end of his strength, as well. *Thank You, Lord, thank You...*

Woodward folded, falling onto his hands. Chest heaving, desperate, wheezing breaths racking his body, he could have been mistaken for the bloody remains of a dog run over by a freight wagon. Jax, breathing like a winded horse himself, spat a mouthful of blood into the dust, took a few more glorious, gulping breaths, then leaned down close to Woodward's ear. "Remember, where...you are...right now." Sucking a deep, invigorating breath, he straightened and staggered over to Woodward's men, and to Cecelia. Chauncey and the others glared at him but did the honorable thing and inched back. "Cecelia..." Jax extended a bloody hand. "Let's go."

Her gaze shot past him and her eyes widened in horror. "Loo—"

Jax started to turn. The revolver in Woodward's hand roared fire and lead.

CHAPTER FIFTEEN

TIME SLOWED. SOUND CEASED. THE AIR AROUND Cecilia turned to a heavy, invisible sludge.

Everything jumbled into nightmarish chaos. Woodward, still on all fours, reached over and snatched Jax's revolver from its holster. She screamed a strangled warning. As the foul man pivoted and fired, Jax was turning to him. At nearly the same instant as Woodward pulled the trigger, a grim-faced Miss Sally rose up from the grass, rifle pressed to her shoulder, and the Winchester thundered, belching fire. Jax spun violently with the impact of Woodward's bullet, blood and tissue spraying the air. Woodward slammed backward onto the ground, sightless eyes staring at the sky.

Cecelia lunged from the porch, clawing through the gunsmoke to cradle Jax's motionless body. Immediately, she felt the hot, sticky liquid coat her fingers. She pulled her hand from beneath his torso. It glistened red. His whole shoulder looked to be a bloody, mangled mess. She could see bone. Around her, more gunfire thundered, but it sounded unreal, muffled, now fading. Chauncey and the others were running. The girls from the Burning Dress firing after them.

"Cecelia?"

Miss Sally's voice snatched Cecelia from the mental fog. She gasped, and the sound of life around her rushed in. Virginia dropped down in front of her, touched her cheek. "You all right?" To Jax. "Is he all right? Oh, Miss Sally, he ain't all right."

The words struck Cecelia like an arrow. "What do you mean? He's going to be fine." With clumsy movements, she attempted to press part of her skirt to his shoulder, but the area was nothing but a raw, gaping wound. "He's going to be fine." He was unconscious. His head lolled in her lap, dark hair falling across his eyes. He was alarmingly pale. "Oh, God…" she whispered, unable to finish the thought.

"Here now, we'll take care of him." Virginia began ripping a swath of cloth from her skirt.

"Maria, Helen." Miss Sally turned, and Cecelia saw several women from the Burning Dress holding smoking rifles and looking on with concern. Maria and Helen stepped forward. "Ride back toward the ranch. Wilhelma shouldn't be that far behind us in the wagon. Get her here pronto."

Cecelia turned back to Jax and wondered at the moisture on his face. Then she realized her tears were dripping onto his cheek. Virginia, with great care and skill, wrapped his shoulder securely with her dress and then squeezed Cecelia's hand. "I need more cloth."

Cloth. To stem the bleeding. Warning bells clanged in her head. Jax could bleed to death. And she very, very much did not want to see that happen. "Here." Gently, she placed his head on the ground and took off her shirt. She handed it to Virginia, then retook her place, cradling Jax's head, ignoring the blood on her camisole. "I don't want anything to happen to him, Virginia."

The girl's hands paused for an instant. "Don't worry. He's gonna be all right." She started adding the wrapping to his injury and muttered under her breath, "Long as Wilhelma don't dally with the wagon."

Cecelia marveled over the sharp, jagged fear she felt for Jax, like glass in the pit of her stomach. She didn't want him to die. She'd do anything to save him. If only she could have stepped in front of Woodward's shot.

She couldn't explain where these feelings had come from. She was as surprised by them as she suspected Jax might be. And they proved one thing to her: maybe she wasn't *in* love with Jax—she didn't know—but she *could* love him. She could, because what frightened her now was that he might die.

Miss Sally crouched beside Jax and laid her hand lightly on his injury. "You will live, Jax. You will not die. Father, I thank You for Your love and mercy and the hedge of protection You have around this boy. This bullet will not take his life. I believe that. I pray for quick healing and..." She glanced at the bloody rags. "Complete healing. He will have the use of his arm. Thank you, Jesus, that by Your stripes Jax is going to be all right—"

"Miss Sally, you're bleeding, too." Virginia reached toward her boss's leg but pulled her hand back.

"Just a flesh wound," the woman said indifferently.

The sound of riders pounding toward the group brought the remaining Burning Dress girls to attention. They cocked their rifles and stared into the gunsmoke. To Cecelia's shock, Sam Hain and Quitman Taylor emerged from it, swinging down off their horses and rushing to Miss Sally.

Hain instantly assessed the situation, coming back to the older woman and noting her injury with a fearsome look of fury. "Are you all right?"

"Yes, it's nothing to worry about."

Taylor stood over Cecelia, staring down at Jax. Mouth agape, breathing heavy, he slowly knelt beside her and laid a hand on Jax's cheek. Then she saw the tears in his eyes.

"What happened?" Hain asked.

"Woodward and his boys decided to take a few of my ranch hands for an afternoon of entertainment. Jax found 'em."

Hain surveyed the man on the ground once more, then studied the trail of blood staining Miss Sally's pants. His handsome face hardened, took on a dangerous, flinty edge. "Time for their reckoning."

Miss Sally's hand shot out and clutched Hain's, resting on the butt of his gun. "No, Sam. Stay out of it. Please. I'm all right. Jax is going to be all right. There's no reason for you to get involved."

"I don't need a reason. You know that." He turned his attention to Taylor. "You stay with your son, Quitman. I'll handle your boys."

Cecelia's eyes widened. *Son?* But the realization was plowed under by the threat in Hain's voice.

Taylor bit down on his knuckles and nodded. "Do what you have to do."

Hain turned to go, but Miss Sally held on. "No. Every time you give in, you slide a little further—"

"Toward hell?" He raised his hand, almost touched her cheek, but shook his head and pulled away. "We both know that's where I'm bound." Before she could say anything else, Hain snatched his arm free and pushed past her.

"No, Sam," she whispered, watching him go. "We don't know that."

"His shoul—" Quitman Taylor tripped on his words. He cleared his throat and tried again, lifting his gaze to Cecelia. "Shoulder. Is it bad?" The older man's chin quivered, and tears pooled in old eyes filled with fear. "That's a lot of blood."

Cecelia actually felt bad for him, in spite of what she knew. A father, either a good or a bad one, could be undone by the sight of his son gravely injured. "He'll be all right. He has to be."

"This is my fault," he said, collapsing on his hip beside his son. "I should never have let him leave the ranch. We should have tried to get past what—what I did."

Miss Sally rested her hand on his shoulder. "Quitman, he had to have time to deal with things. Do a little growing up. Seems to me, you had a little growing up to do, too."

"I musta been out of my mind chasing after that little French trollop. Worse, I shoulda never let her come between my boy and me." He hung his head. "I am a philandering old fool."

"Live and learn, Quitman," Miss Sally said gently. "Live and learn. He'll survive this. And maybe you two can start over."

Cecelia bit down on her lip, kept the pressure on Jax's wound, and prayed to God that Miss Sally was right.

CHAPTER SIXTEEN

TWIRLING HER STETSON IN HER HAND, SALLY STEPPED out onto the porch in front of Doc's and released a deep sigh. Jax's shoulder was a mess, but Doc Adams was a fine surgeon. Her foreman would be fine, but the recovery would be long. Regardless, he was alive, and she was grateful. "Thank you, Jesus," she whispered aloud.

And she believed in her heart that more healing was to come. Jax and his father would reconcile. There had been no mistaking the regret in Taylor's eyes, and Jax was not hard-hearted. He would forgive a foolish old man frightened of his mortality.

Would Jax, however, go back to the Bar T? Sally couldn't say. Judging by Cecelia's concern for their foreman, she suspected the girl may figure into his choices. "At least, I hope so, Lord. I think they can be good for each other."

Whatever direction things went for the two of them, Sally was encouraged, and she nodded to herself. The wistful smile on her lips, however, faded abruptly when she looked up the street and saw Sam riding in. Her heart clenched in pain. He was leading three horses, limp bodies slung over the saddles, dead arms swaying with the animals' trot. She sucked in a breath to steady herself.

She couldn't even pray it had been an accident or self-defense. She knew better.

Sam and his train of death trudged up to the doc's office. He took a second before he met her gaze. Sally tried to hold back the tears, but they escaped with unstoppable determination.

He shook his head and snorted softly in disgust. "You do to this to yourself." He swiped a dirty hand over his jaw, scratched at the unkempt stubble distorting his perfect beard. "I am what I am, and I'm good at it." There was no pride in the declaration, something quite the opposite, in fact.

Such regret was always what made her hope rear up. "And I have the faith you'll change. I'll pray for you until the Second Coming."

He shook his head and rapped his knuckles on the saddle horn. Seconds of painful silence ticked by. "Technically, it was self-defense. I let them shoot first."

This time, she snorted softly at the abysmal defense but didn't comment further. He sighed and nudged the horse. Sally closed her eyes and listened to the weary horses' steps fade away.

JAX LEANED his head back into the thin pillow and stared up at the ceiling. His shoulder felt as if he'd been stepped on by a Brahma bull. Correction. The bull was still there doing the Mexican Hat Dance. Beside him, Taylor sat bouncing a leg and twirling his hat. His father was so fidgety, Jax thought if he had plates, he'd be spinning them. "You're making me nervous," he complained. "Get hold of yourself."

Taylor breathed slowly but loudly for a few minutes, then he swallowed, the sound too loud in the small examination room. "You-you feeling all right?"

"Doc says I'll make it."

"The shoulder?"

Jax eyed the bandages for a moment, pondered the pain. How was he supposed to work hemmed up like this? "A long recovery, but I should be all right in a few months." Months.

Taylor cleared his throat. "You could-you could recover at home. If you were of a mind to."

Jax looked at his father then. Really looked at him. The gray had taken over nearly all of the brown hair. The creases around the man's eyes were etched deeper. More surprisingly, his gaze was weary and defeated. He seemed smaller now, as well. As if life had kicked the bluster and swagger right out him.

"I think you must look worse than I do. You sick?"

Taylor snorted, shook his head. "Only with myself. Took almost losing you to bring me around."

The candid answer surprised Jax and left him scrambling for a response. He didn't know what to say, especially since that wasn't an apology exactly.

But he owed his father one. No matter who had done what to whom. "That fight should have never happened. It grieves me to think of it. I'm ashamed."

Taylor sighed heavily and hung his head. "You got nothing to be sorry for. I deserved a whooping, acting the fool over a girl not even half my age. She nearly cost me the only thing I've ever cared about." He looked up at Jax with an intensity of hope that made him ache. He missed his father.

"I don't expect you can understand this, son, but I'm seventy. Your ma's been gone a decade. Pauline... Pauline..."

"Made you feel young?"

"She sure made me think my last breath was a little farther off than it is. And the girls at Sam's Place. I'm just trying to outrun the Grim Reaper."

Jax supposed growing old alone and with no hope of something better on the other side was enough to scare a man senseless. Witless if a beautiful woman came along to tempt you.

"I think you're doing a sight better with Cecelia."

His head snapped up. "What?"

Taylor studied Jax for a moment before cutting loose with a big, silly grin. "She's been here the whole time. Two days. Didn't leave once. Until now. To let me sit with you and go get cleaned up."

Jax was taken aback. He didn't know how he felt about this news. Before the fight with Woodward, Jax had told her he was fighting for more than reasons of brotherly love. He'd felt compelled to say something... if the fight didn't go in his favor. In the heat of the moment, he hadn't thought of how to deal with the aftermath. What had he done? *Lord, what now...?*

"Anyway..." Taylor cleared his throat. "I needed to tell you I'm sorry. More sorry than I can say. And I hope you'll"—he paused, worked his jaw around for a second—"hope you'll forgive me. I understand if you don't want to come back, but the Bar T will always be your home."

Jax's thoughts were tumbling over themselves as his father stood and trudged toward the door. Bent and weary. The image brought him up short. "Pa." How long since he'd called him that?

Taylor turned, hat in his hands, pressed humbly to his chest.

"Someday I'll be seventy, Lord willing, and I might let a pretty girl twist me up in knots, too." He dipped his chin, signaling forgiveness, and his father smiled.

"No, son, not you. You always were smarter than me." With a brave wink, he slipped out the door.

In the quiet room, Jax pondered the storm of emotions swirling in his heart. A weight had been lifted off him. He and his father had taken steps to heal the wounds they'd inflicted on each other...and themselves. Jax knew he could risk it. He had the *courage* to risk it.

But when it came to Cecelia, well, he wasn't sure at all what to do with her. He closed his eyes and set to praying.

Cecelia was exhausted. Downright dead to the bone. She'd spent two days sitting beside Jax, watching over him, her mind a blur of wild, jumbled thoughts, questions, and emotions. She had feelings for him. And didn't know what to do with them. He might have feelings for her. And she had prayed for his recovery. Prayed. Now, she wanted to know how did she find God? Had He heard her prayers? Who could tell her? Where did she start? Was the prayer born of desperation? But she'd never sought the Lord's help at any time during her failing marriage. Something about Burning Dress, the people, Miss Sally, brought God closer...

And shouldn't she get back to work? Surely her boss might be wondering...Mr. Taylor's arrival had seemed the time to depart. She'd slipped away without a word to Jax because she simply didn't know what to say. And, besides, speaking with his father was more important than anything she might have to say...

She rode Twister into the barn, both of them moving as if they were stuck in molasses. Molly came from somewhere and stopped the horse. "You look like you been rode hard and put up wet."

Cecelia couldn't muster the energy to laugh but offered a weak smile.

Molly reached for the reins. "Here, I'll put him up. You go inside." As Cecelia climbed down, Molly asked, "Jax? He's all right?"

"He was awake when I left, but"—she arched her back, wincing at the stiffness—"I didn't speak to him.

His father had come by. He was going to offer to let Jax recuperate at the Bar T."

Molly's eyes widened. "He'd leave us for the Bar T?"

"Taylor is his father, I guess you heard. It would be right."

Molly started leading the horse away. "I suppose, but I'd say we'd all be better nurses than those fools there."

Perhaps, Cecelia thought, but irrelevant at the moment. Jax needed healing for more than his shoulder, and the Bar T was the place to start the process.

She trudged toward the main house, but the porch on the saddle shop looked so inviting. She could hear Virginia humming from inside. Cecelia gave in to the urge to check on her friend and rest on the front porch. With effort, she managed to sit rather than collapse and called over her shoulder, "Virginia."

The girl's humming stopped instantly, and she rushed to the door. Cecelia gave her a weak smile.

"Holy Joe, you look like something the cat dragged in." In two steps, she was kneeling beside Cecelia. "Can I get you anything? Water?"

"A stretcher." Cecelia lay back, removing her hat and setting it on her chest. "I might need the help getting to my bed."

She heard the shifting of fabric beside her and assumed Virginia had settled more comfortably. "You stayed at Doc's two whole days. Jax gonna be all right?"

"I think so." And before the girl could ask, Cecelia

said, "And I think he's going to do his recovery at the Bar T." A prolonged silence prompted Cecelia to open one eye to peer at Virginia. "You've nothing to say to that?"

She screwed her face up into an expression of great contemplation. "Those of us who haven't been here long didn't know Taylor is his pa. It's fittin', I guess."

"I guess." But what did this mean for Cecelia...and Jax? If there was an *and*. Frustrated, tired of the circular thoughts, she forced herself up on her elbows, then to a sitting position. "Nothing has turned out here like I thought it would, Virginia." She bounced her hat in her hands for a moment, then dropped it on her head.

"Meaning?"

Cecelia shook her head. "William hurt me. More than I was willing to admit. He made me afraid of letting anyone in. And now I worry about you, hoping you'll be happy. And when Woodward and Jax were fighting...I prayed." Embarrassed, she turned her gaze to Virginia and grinned sheepishly at her friend's wide, brown eyes filled with unabashed happiness. Cecelia shrugged. "Yes, I prayed. But I don't understand why...or Who even. I just felt this emptiness and reached out."

"Scripture says only a fool says in his heart there is no God." Virginia dropped an arm around Cecelia. "You ain't no fool. And it sounds to me like He used a moment when you couldn't fix things yourself to bring the truth home."

Cecelia thought perhaps Virginia was a lot smarter than she let on. "So, now what?"

"Now I get to tell you the part about God putting on flesh and becoming one of us. To die for us."

"Why, Virginia, why would He do that?"

Virginia smiled and hugged Cecelia tighter, knocking off her hat. "I think it's because He knew we'd be worth it."

CHAPTER SEVENTEEN

JAX SLEPT FITFULLY ON AND OFF FOR THE NEXT FOUR days. Taylor came to visit him every day, and father and son began rebuilding their relationship. But as things warmed with his father, Jax wondered more and more about Cecelia. If she'd stayed with him two days straight, where was she now? Why hadn't she come back to see him, check on him? He'd prayed for clarity on his feelings for her, dreamed about her over and over, and wished for a chance to talk with her. But she hadn't come by Doc's for that to happen.

Then again, no one from the Burning Dress Ranch had come to see him. Not Miss Sally, Molly, any of the girls. Not even Lowdy. Jax was on the verge of hurt feelings when his pa entered, carrying some clothes.

"Doc says you can go home today. I brought you some fresh duds."

A weight, one of several, lifted off Jax. "I'm ready to get out of here, that's for sure."

Taylor laid the clothes at the foot of the bed. "You,

uh, given any thought to my offer about coming back to the Bar T?"

"Yeah, I have. And I would like to come home and heal up."

"That's good. That's good to hear." Taylor let out a long breath and nodded.

"But I'm not sure I'm staying, Pa. I need to talk to Miss Sally." *And Cecelia.*

His father didn't look offended. "Miss Sally has come by a couple of times this week to check on you," he said, dropping into the chair beside the bed. "But she didn't want to wake you."

Jax sucked on his cheek thoughtfully. He felt some better. "Miss Sally, huh? Nobody else?"

Mischief twinkled in Taylor's eyes, and his brow lifted slightly. "That other gal has come by a time or two. She wouldn't wake you, either."

Jax felt good about going home. But he still had some other plans to hammer out. With an arm that felt as strong as a wet noodle, he pushed the blanket off and dropped his feet over the edge. "Let's go home."

JAX DRUMMED his fingers on the coffee table and stared at the note. He'd sent two letters in the last week inviting Cecelia to visit him at the Bar T. Both times, she had responded with a version of, *Thank you, but I can't get away at this time. We're simply overwhelmed at the ranch right now and short-handed.*

He picked up his coffee cup, brought it to his lips, but set it back down. *She's not a Believer, Lord. Maybe I just need to let her go. It's not like I had her in the first place. But I wanted a chance—*

"Jax," his father yelled from downstairs. "Jax, Miss Sally is here to see you."

Jax huffed. Yes. Good. Just who he needed to see. He would ask her straight-up for some advice on Cecelia. He hurried downstairs, trying not to jostle his sling-wrapped shoulder, and found her in the library. "Miss Sally, good to see you."

She placed an affectionate kiss on his cheek. "And you. We surely miss you at the Burning Dress."

He ducked his chin and wandered over to the fireplace. "How are things?"

"Well, I was enjoying my semi-retirement, Jax, I won't lie. With you being hemmed up like you are, I'm back to working some long days."

He cut his eyes at her and grinned. "And you love it."

"I don't hate it. But I'd like time to do some other things, which is why I'm here. I was wondering if you've made any decisions. I know it'll be another month or so before you can even get in the saddle, but the job is open for you until you say different."

Jax hung his head and studied the bandage that immobilized his arm. "Cecelia implied you're pretty busy. I've asked her to come for a visit twice, and she's turned me down both times."

"Jax..." Miss Sally sort of meandered across the room, drifting her hand over the back of the settee, joining him at the hearth. "How much does she figure into your decision?"

He shrugged. "To be honest, as far as where I work, she doesn't." *Not much, anyway.* "My father needs me. I think more than you do."

She smiled, and he thought she looked relieved. "I understand. And I don't disagree. I'll make Lowdy foreman. I've thought about it for years. He'll do fine."

"Yes, he will." Jax rubbed his neck, ran his fingers through his hair. "Speaking of Cecelia…you know, I… I could…" He sighed heavily, swiped a hand over his mouth. "I'm struggling there, Miss Sally. I'd really like to-to…but I can't repeat Pauline. I don't want anything or anyone to turn me from the Lord again, but Cecelia…she's not…I don't know…maybe I could ask her if—"

"Jax." Miss Sally laid a hand on his chest, stopping him, mercifully. "I don't know what you're trying to say, but I have a message for you from Cecelia." She pulled a folded piece of paper from her back pocket and handed it to him.

Frowning, he opened it slowly to discover it was a sheet of music. *Annie Laurie.* He looked up.

"It's Friday night. Baxter's tuning up his fiddle." She squeezed his hand in goodbye, took a few steps toward the door, then stopped. "One more thing you need to know, Jax." She glanced over her shoulder. "Cecelia burned her wedding dress last night."

Her smile spreading, Miss Sally winked and let herself out.

Jax went back to the paper in his hand.

Annie Laurie...
Just one dance?

THE MERE THOUGHT of the Friday night festivities made Cecelia's mouth go dry. What if he didn't show up? She sat in front of the mirror, pulling a brush through her long, auburn tresses. She hadn't been in a dress since their one-and-only dance. Sadly, she was wearing the same blue dress he'd already seen.

"You look mighty pretty." Virginia's reflection grinned at her in the mirror. "Maybe you'll get more than one dance out of him tonight."

Cecelia dropped her gaze. "And what if I do?" She shook her head. "I'm overwhelmed, Virginia. I thought I was confused when William tossed me out on my ear. I couldn't believe I turned into a cowboy. I still have so much to learn about Jesus. And, now, here I am hoping Jax..." She didn't finish because she didn't know what she was hoping for exactly.

Virginia laid her hand on Cecelia's shoulder. "You're a smart girl, 'Celia. And Jax ain't no dummy. You'll figure it out."

"What if he doesn't come tonight?" The sheet music surely was a clear enough invitation. What if it implied too much?

"He'll show."

"How did you know?" Cecelia asked into the mirror. She'd never said one word to Virginia or anyone other than Miss Sally about her attraction to Jax. "About my feelings for Jax, I mean."

At first, Virginia's big, round eyes widened even more, then she settled back with a chuckle. "Couldn't have been more obvious if you'd both worn signs."

"Both? You think he…?"

"Oh, yes, sister. That boy is smitten. Don't make him brave, though." She winked into the mirror. "But I suspect he is."

BUT BY THE time Baxter pulled out his fiddle, Jax still had not joined them. Cecelia's spirits began to flag, and her interest in checkers as well. The sound of shuffling feet increased as the cowboys on loan from their wives pulled a few of the girls to their feet. Wilhelma reached across the table and shook Cecelia with gruff but sincere affection. "Don't be downcast. He vill show."

Virginia slid a checker forward. "She's right. Have a little faith."

At that moment, Cecelia looked up, and her breath caught in her throat. Jax was standing a few feet away, wearing a new black suit, a hefty, black sling around his left arm and shoulder, and a mischievous grin. He pulled the coat back and rested a hand on his hip. His soft black hair curled a little at his collar. Blue eyes that flickered with invitation and alluring confidence sent her pulse sky high.

"Dance with me, Cecelia." He extended his hand to her.

She didn't move, and after a moment, Wilhelma nudged her firmly, snapping Cecelia out of her daze. Baxter struck up a lively rendition of a schottische, and Jax wiggled his fingers. Biting down a grin, Cecelia took his hand and let him and the music take her away. Happiness perfected in this one, single moment exploded in her heart, and she determined not to think past it.

Holding hands, they stepped, and hopped—gently—and side-stepped, Cecelia's laughter bubbling up at her rusty familiarity with the waltz and Jax's awkwardness with one arm. His soothing, gentle voice directing her steps, and his light touch on her hip as they paraded around the floor, was intoxicating. She looked up into his alluring gaze and unexpectedly thought, *I could dance with him forever, Lord...*

His step faltered, but his grin widened. "I think you're getting the hang of it."

"You know, I think I am." But Cecelia didn't think either of them was referring to the dance. Something in her breathed deeply, freely, majestically. Her spirit soared. "I'm happy. For the first time in a very long time, I am happy. And I feel so lighthearted." Yes, Jax had something to do with it, but he was more the icing on the cake than the substance of her joy.

Baxter finished off the schottische and wiped perspiration off his brow. "How 'bout I slow things down a bit so's I can catch my breath?"

He shifted into a melancholy version of *Streets of*

Laredo, and Jax pulled Cecelia close, deftly using one good arm to lead her in the slow waltz. His broad, muscled chest, penetrating blue eyes, and a tender smile were thieves. He could steal her breath if she let him. "I'm glad you came." She gently clutched the fingers hanging free of the sling, slid her other hand up to his neck.

"About that. I've been doing a ton of thinking, 'Celia." He watched her face as if looking for a clue to her thoughts. "My pa's health isn't so good, and I'm obviously gonna be recovering for a while. I won't be coming back to the Burning Dress as the foreman."

"I know. Miss Sally told us."

They danced a few minutes in a silence filled only with Baxter's weeping fiddle and their own ruminations. After several steps, he said, "She told me you burned your dress."

"Not all of it. Only the veil and the bodice. I gave the rest to Virginia. She's going to make angel gowns from it."

He nodded with satisfaction. "Now, I like that idea."

"And I went to church. Twice. Miss Sally's teaching a Bible study. I've been attending that as well."

Jax inclined his head, as if this news interested him keenly. "And? What do you think?"

A broad question, she supposed, but the answer, born of deep gratitude, caused tears to moisten her eyes. "I am not worthless if my Savior would die for me. William was wrong." She stared off into the crowd and blinked away the emotions before they spilled openly down her cheeks, but she was so grateful to be free from the lies. "I can't even hear his voice anymore."

They stopped moving. His warm hand tilted her gaze back up to him. "Good. I don't want you to."

She looked at him, puzzled by his husky, determined tone.

"No one is ever going to talk to you like that again. You're a treasure. You should be treated like one."

Cecelia drank in the compliment, amazed at the emotions such kind, beautiful words stirred in her. They were like a balm, like warm oil, cascading over her whole being, healing, reviving. Again, her eyes welled up, and Jax started them dancing again, perhaps so she could regain her composure. The power of words—*his* words—moved her deeply.

"One good thing about Pauline Lautrec," he said, looking past her. "She taught me the difference between love and lust." He furtively danced her over to a quiet corner and brought them to a standstill. Sighing, he lifted his hand to her cheek again. "I don't want this to be just one dance, Cecelia."

Oh, how his eyes glimmered with a steadiness and strength that made her want to believe him. "I'm afraid, you know. Everything has changed in my life—all in a good way, but I'm still afraid of being hurt."

Jax slid his arm around her and pulled her against him, his fingers caressing the hollow of her back. His broad chest beneath her fingers was solid, reliable. The tenderness in his expression sent fire shooting from the top of her head to the soles of her feet. Oh, but this fire was inviting, warm, and comforting. It wouldn't flare up brilliantly hot, only to consume her and leave nothing behind but ashes. This fire would last. It would never burn her.

"I want to love you, Cecelia, and honor you, and protect you. And we'll take it as slow as you want. I'm not going anywhere." He searched her face, waiting. "Don't let fear stop you from living, from letting someone into your life who *will* cherish you."

Could she? Could she just fling all her fear to the wind?

No.

But she could cast it on the cross.

"You said, 'Faith or fear. I can't have both.'" Her breath coming in short gasps, her heartbeat careening wildly, Cecelia faced the edge of the cliff and stepped off. She clutched his lapel. "I choose faith. Faith in Him…and faith in you."

Jax exhaled, as if he'd been holding his breath. He leaned down and pressed a gentle kiss to Cecelia's lips, a kiss full of promise and longing and breathless passion. Joy blazed in her soul. "I feel like a princess," she whispered.

Jax kissed her nose, her mouth, then drifted his lips to her ear. "You are, darlin'. You are."

THANK YOU

Thank you for reading *A Distant Heart.* I hope you loved this story as much as I do. If you have the time, I'd love if you could share a review on Amazon.

ABOUT THE AUTHOR

Heather Blanton is a *USA Today* bestselling author of thirty Christian Western romances, including the highly rated and awarded Romance in the Rockies series. She is also an award-winning script writer. Her Romance in the Rockies series has been optioned for a limited TV series, and her script *Unbridled Hearts* is currently optioned as well.

She grew up in the mountains of Western North Carolina on a steady diet of *Bonanza, Gunsmoke,* and John Wayne Westerns. Her daddy taught her to shoot when she was five, and she can hit that at which she aims.

Her novels are all Christian Western romance because she enjoys creating feisty pioneer women who struggle to find love and hold on to their faith. Like all good, old-fashioned Westerns, there is always justice, a moral message, American values, lots of high adventure, unexpected plot twists, and often a touch of suspense.

www.authorheatherblanton.com

www.ingramcontent.com/pod-product-compliance
Lightning Source LLC
LaVergne TN
LVHW040219110826
845146LV00005B/1343

* 9 7 9 8 8 9 5 6 7 8 4 0 4 *